WHEN HEROES FALL

SHARAN RIVAS

Contents

Chapter 1

I never knew my parents.

I know, it sounds like every villain story, but this is "different".

And it goes like this,

Everyone believes that the heroes were amazing.

They got all the sha-bang.

But only the ones, who didn't get brainwashed know it's all a game.

They are using us.

It's there little game they love to play, its called who can get manipulated the quickest.

Well, that's what I have been told, but seeing it with my eyes is worse.

The heroes, they are the definition of two faced.

Let me rephrase that, they are two faced and just a bunch of posers.

And they're hurting my people.

My people , who don't get a chance to tell their side of the story.

If you're not brain-washed yet, then the heroes will find you and kill you.

All I'm saying is,

I didn't grow up wanting to help everyone I see, that needs help.

Some people don't need other people's help.

Sky, lily, yelled "what are you doing in there, you're gonna be late".

"Coming", I said loud and clear.

Lily, is one of my closest friends and sorta my only, oh who am I kidding, she is my only friend.

She's like a big sister I never had.

I walked out of my room and said, "what do you need now"? "my lungs, my kidney"

"no", she said I have an assignment for you.

"what is it" I asked.

"We need to take back what was ours".

"and whats that exactly"I said confused

"umm", a vile she said bluntly.

"Why"?

"Rob needs it to finish his masterpiece", she said, rolling her eyes.

"He's still working on that thing"?

"hey", she said that thing, is to get us loads of money, in the black market.

I rolled my eyes, "of course, always for the money".

"huh", do you want to starve.

"I wasn't planning on it", so, "what's my mission" I asked, kinda annoyed.

"well", how should I put this.

"We need you to go to a party".

"No", I said, I hate parties with a passion, you know that.

"I know, but that's where the deal is gonna take place".

"We need you to take it", and bring it back.

"Fine", I said "ok, great" she said "lets pick out a dress for you".

"yeah", I said totally, beaming with happiness. not.

She pulled me into her room and placed me on her bed, "alright," she said while getting a dress from her closet.

I need you to also get info about the W.C.H (means world class heroes).

Smart huh, well ours is W.C.V. with a V nothing too special, but we prefer to be called the outcast as are bad guy name.

"That's why you are making me go to the party"? "don't be so dense", about this she said .

"Now, try on this dress".

I changed in the closet and when I got out lily said gosh Skylare you're so cute.

"Thanks", I said trying to keep myself from smiling.

So, I am going to the party, get the vile, then boom leave.
"Yes"she said, also keep in mind, it will be packed with the heroes, so, keep watch.

What is this party even for?

For the showing of the new vile ding dong.

And so you want me to go and take it?

"Yes", we already talked about this, they are going to show it to the new groups.

"yeah", but you do know its gonna be packed with the heroes right?

"yeah", lily smiled but you got it right?

"Mmh", I said.

And how is this taking back what is ours?

Because they took jasper.

My body froze.

jasper, I repeated

lily nodded

Jasper, was one of the best scientists ever to be alive.

And he was also a father figure in some cases.

It sounded cheesy but its so true.

They took his formula and changed it.

Isn't that stealing.

not in their rule book, it's fine for them to take, but when it involves helping others, they take from the outcast group.

but we haven't stirred up to much trouble?

why? are they messing with us now.

"because, they have us on a short leash and we are like dogs to them" lily huffed.

I nodded "preach it sister".

"So tonight we take back what is ours" she smirked at me.

I nodded.

I'm ready to go.

great lets head out.

I got up and said goodbye to rob.

We drove to the headquarters that I thought I wouldn't go back to.

I got out and said "wish me luck".

"Oh wait", lily said, Take this flower.

"Why", I said.

Because, it shows that you are a part of the W.C.H. "cool", I said.

I ran up to the familiar steps.

Walked in and a guy asked "who are you"? and "what's your powers"?

I lied and said, "Um, combat and engineering", he checked the list.

You are in soul group, "where is your flower to represent"?

I showed him, He nodded.

I went in.

I muttered, "this is it Skylare.

CHAPTER 2

I found my group and there were two girls and three guys.

That's when all the memories hit.

It's Conrad, Scarelett, Amber and mark.

But who's the other guy?

I walked over and i said, "hi my name is sky".

Conrad said, "hi I'm the leader of this group".

But before he could finish, Scarelett had to cut in and say, "who are you"? "we don't need outsiders like you".

"Scarlett", Conrad said trying to sound mad, but i knew him as the softest guy you could ever meet. "She is new so show her some respect".

I nodded, they didn't recognize me.

What's your name? again, "sky".

Then Conrad said the weirdest thing, "is that a short name for Skylare".

"NO", i said quickly, "its just sky", "Interesting" Scarelett said, while giving me the eye, that i know is never good.

Coming from her, it's like a death threat.

"Come, sit down with us", Conrad said, trying to get me out of the awkward situation.

I sat in the middle of scarelett and Conrad.

She was always suspicious of anything.

"So, how did you get in"? she said, cocky.

"Doesn't it take um, what's the word", "skill to join a group like ours"?

Man, I thought, when she get so cocky about everything, never mind that, she was always mean and cocky.

"Well", it's not that hard getting in".

"If they let you in".

She sneered, "you little"- she huffed.

Point Skylare, zero Scarelett, "No", Conrad said trying to get me out of an argument, even though i knew i could win.

"So what are your skills"? "you're gonna bring in this group"?

"Well, i'm pretty good at combat", "and i dabble in some engineering ,"so, yeah".

"So, what I'm hearing is that , you're practically human", scarelett ,said.

Does she ever shut up, i thought.

"No, not exactly", i said smiling. But that smile, quickly turned into a sneer.

"What do you mean", she asked.

"I'm not sure"?

"Guys",amber chimed, "be nice she's new, and maybe freaked out, about this whole new atmosphere? she is gonna make".

"Well", mark said, I am gonna get food, cause, that's the only reason I wanted to come.

He was getting up, when Amber said, "wait, for me mark", they got close.

I thought they hated each other, when I was around, but then again, I was only 12.

I had no clue, what love really was.

And still today, I'm pretty clueless, in the area of love.

So,nothing really changed, much about me.

"So", Conrad said, trying not to make the group feel more awkward, which he is already doing by doing the awkward sigh.

"So", he said again, but this time to me.

What does he think he's doing, dragging me into this?

"Do you know about the new thing that they are making"? "It's so cool how the scientist finally made a breakthrough".

"What" i said, bewildered at what my ears just heard.

"Yeah", Conrad said, the scientists have been working their butt's off, trying to make a breakthrough.

"Woah" i said, um, "so what does this vile do exactly"?

"I don't know exactly, but I can't wait".

Well, i know, Scarelett beamed.

"How"? Conrad said.

"Well my dad is the one who helped with the breakthrough".

Of course, she and her dad are like the most prideful people that could ever walk the earth.

That's cool, Conrad said.

"Yes, i know, I hate those pricks of an outcast".

I rolled my eyes , note to myself: remind me to puncture her with the vile in her sleep.

"Finally, we can take down the outcast once and for all".

Then there will be no more bad guys.

Clearly she doesn't understand that the world isn't sunshine and rainbows?

"Wait, what happens to the bad guys"?

"They will lose their powers and probably be put in a place for the mentally insane".

I gulped, "why? so nervous", a voice across from me asked.

I looked at him. He looked attractive, I guess? he had blonde curly hair, that went well with his pretty hazel eyes.

That could make you get lost in them for hours.

I wasn't planning on doing that...but, the thought is still there.

He's giving, mysterious.

"Me, nervous" I scoffed "yes, you", he said, while rolling his eyes.

"Why? so jittery"

" It's nothing for you to worry about"

He narrowed his eyes, but didn't say anything.

What a weirdo.

The only reason I was like this was because, they stole something that clearly didn't belong to them.

They lied, claiming, that they worked their butts off, making the vile, it just gets my blood boiling.

The so-called heroes are supposed to keep this fake city safe.

like I said, they are just asking for chaos , if they think using a vile that takes away our powers will do something.

Think again, heroes

And besides we haven't started anything bad enough that they needed to destroy the whole outcast.

But I guess that's just how it works: villian's never win in any story. "Um sky", Conrad said, "you alive, or what?

I got out of my trance and said "I'm doing great".

"Good, cause the thing is about to start".

I looked up and saw the heads of the council.

Rick, Steven and Scott oh, wait, and don't forget about Barbara.

She was always a funny person, whenever she was mad.

I'm not trying to be proud or anything but, I could easily destroy her in a fight.

Then we finally heard the order and I stopped thinking.

"Ladies and gents we are finally proud to show you the thing we've been working on for the past few years".

Cap.

He unveiled the cloth that was on it.

"Now, I present to you the one and only thing that can take down the outcast".

I smell something fishy and filled with cap.

you can never take down the outcasts.

we've been though heck and back, living like a fungus that wont go away

that was a weird analogy but...

am I wrong?

How am I supposed to get the vile, without them knowing that I took it.

He just said it's the one and only.

"Ok ladies and gents I will now show you what this baby can do".

"Bring in prisoner 66".

Oh, Scarelett smiled, that prisoner deserves to get his powers wiped.

But when they brought in the prisoner, my heart sank.

"No, I whispered it cant be".

Jasper, was the outcast that was gonna pay.

CHAPTER 3

Everyone clapped, for joy, even my group was smiling. I felt like my heart was about to break, and my bones were already shaking.

"We'll put the vile in him, the liquid will seep through his veins, killing him slowly", rick said.

"But, that's only for the worst villian's that truly deserve it, rick said.

That is why, Jasper Kevin's, is here, with us today.

I shook my head.

This can't be, I thought, he didn't even do anything, he doesn't even kill.

He was a father to me, and I won't stand for this crap.

I stood up and said, "um, excuse me" all eyes were on me.

But i didn't care, this was my father figure, they were about to kill.

"Um, yes, you, girl what is it you need?"

"How many people did jasper Kevin kill?"

"What does that have to do, with this, girl".

"Well, shouldn't the victim that killed people be the ones who get the vile?"

"Yes, that's what he is here for, silly girl," Rick smiled.

"No, but jasper doesn't kill, he is an evil scientist he only experiments, no killing involved in being a scientist".

"So, why, are you testing it on a villian that should only be in jail, for his crimes"?

He never would kill anyone, because he wouldn't have time to commit any murder's.

"Well", Scott said baffled.

"But, he is the most wanted criminal in the city, and i don't think your reasons are well,   reasonable".

That's just the heroes saying your right, just, I don't like how you're right,..

typical hero, gas-lighting

"He is a psychopath", he chuckled, and you surely can't fix, crazy.

The rest of the groups started whispering.

"silent", Rick said, he then turned to Jasper and smiled, "its time Jasper Kevin's".

I looked at jasper and i mouthed sorry.

He smiled, at me, only to me.

That was then the day, I saw, my father figure, die.

Slow, painful death.

It was sad, it was painful, and devastating.

Jasper didn't deserve to die, he was just a middle aged guy, living in a messed up world.

After the death, of my sorta father, I sat there scared, that was what was gonna happen to everyone that was in the outcast group.

I have to steal that vile tonight.

I was in mid- thinking when amber poked my side, and said, "you remind me of someone".

"Who", i said, not wanting to blow my cover.

Her name was umm...

"Skylare", the mysterious boy chimed in.

"Yeah", amber said, all bubbly, skylare, "oh, how i missed her".

"What happened to her anyways"?, amber pondered

"Well",Conrad said, she left a note saying she can't do it anymore.

"Which was strange, because I thought she loved it here" he said , sadly.

If only they knew my intentions.

I seriously don't give a crap about this place.

It was just a reminder that even the heroes, can't save the world.

"Yeah, maybe she couldn't deal with being the lead leader", scarelett retorted.

omygosh can't she ever shut up, for a sec

Who, said she couldn't deal with it, i just couldn't take it anymore, i had to lead the combat group

While only being the age of, thirteen.

And i already got the information I needed, so there was no point, in me staying.

"Well she kinda dragged us down, during the missions" Scarelett said, reassuring everyone.

I was the one slowing us down?

She must have had some sort of accident, during one of her missions.

Cause i remember it clearly, it was her dragging us down.

"Gosh", Mark said, is that all you really think about when you remember her?

"Yes", Scarelett said,"it also saddens me that she would leave like that".

I just didn't need you guys anymore i said, to myself.

"Well, i said, try not to cry, from all the pain cause , well my father figure,, just died, a painful death.

"Um this been fun, but i need to head out".

"Oh, Scarelett said, we will all miss you so much".

I rolled my eyes, save it for the priest, and i walked out.

CHAPTER 4

I walked home because clearly lily forgot about me. typical day for me, really.

When I finally got to my run down house, that I call home, I walked in and said, "I'm home".

I saw, lily and Rob waiting for me.

oh, so she can wait for me, but not pick me up.

They asked, "how was it".

I gave them both cold looks.

"What happened", lily said, concerned.

"They killed Jasper", I said in a, low voice.

"He was the tester for the vile" I said, frustrated

"Oh, and the vile they used, was his own creation".

"They took it", Rob said, annoyed.

"I knew that something was off, lily said.

"Same", rob chimed in.

"There was just no way, that the heroes knew how to make, a highly powerful vile that could kill".

Also, "I couldn't get it cause they were guarding it like a dog".

"Well then plan B, it is", lily sighed.

"We need that vile, before another war breaks out", lily said, firmly

"We don't want to repeat history", "do we now"?

"Yeah", Rob said, a lot of good people died that day.

"May they rest in peace", Lily, huffed.

"Maybe we should give up".

"No", lily said, "you are the daughter of Lola and Kane".

"Excuse me", "what did you just say to me"?

"Oh, lily said, no one told you the story.

"There's a story"?

"please tell"

"Well, Lola and Kane were enemies to lovers".

"Your mom was part of the combat group".

"That's the group your brother is leading, right now".

"And the group your leading is your fathers, the destruction group".

"They first weren't big fans of each other".

"But they realized, they were gonna have to get used to each other".

"Because, they were gonna be the ones who saved the outcast from the war, the heroes put on us".

"I thought, we were the ones who started the war"?

"That's where you have it all wrong", lily said.

"The heroes didn't like that both outcast groups joined together".

"Cause, they always have to keep us on a short leash", I said, to myself.

"Then your brother was born, then you.

"They realized that the prophecy was true".

"Two, great leaders, joining together, to destroy, the heroes, one day".

"But the heroes didn't like the prophecy".

"So, they killed Lola and Kane.

"Hoping, to destroy any more offspring, that would have come".

"But the worst part was, that your mother, she was expecting, a child".

"No", I said, I would have been an older sister.

Lily nodded, slowly.

"How, do you know" about that?

"Well, lily said, my mom was the one, who brought back the news".

"She was heartbroken, to see the best outcasts couple to ever reign, die sad death".

"They fought for their lives that day, just to protect their children", from the horrible heroes.

"This is terrible", I muttered.

"I will, get my revenge, somehow".

"I will ruin them", I said, angrily.

"They killed my parents, they took everything away from me, my little sister too".

"Its cute how they think, that the kids, wouldn't follow in their parents'footsteps, I sneered.

"Tonight we take the vile"

"You really are the daughter, of Lola and Kane".

"But your driving me there".

I'm not walking, like I did tonight.

I got changed before we left, as I walked out of my room lily smiled and said, "ready".

I smiled and said, "I was born ready".

We got in the car and were off.

We finally got to the headquarters and I said, "ok, when I go in there, you have to tell me, if there is gonna be someone."

We don't want to recap of last time.

"It was an accident I was hoping you would forget" lily said, with a sheepish smile.

"I almost died", I yelled.

"Ok, geeze" your alive ,right?

"My bad", she said, oh, "and don't get recognized".

We haven't been the best outcast lately.

"I thought we were doing great",I smirked.

lily rolled her eyes, and said ,"just be careful".

I know, "stay low , no noise what so ever".

"Good, now, go before someone sees this sketchy car".

I rolled my eyes, and left the sketchy car.

I ran up the stairs and climbed into the window.

"I'm in", I said into the earpiece.

I walked in and there were security cameras everywhere.

"Hey, um, lily could you be a dear, and turn off the cameras".

"Oh, yes", she said.

"All clear", she said.

I went into the room where the vile should be.

I looked around the room and there were no security cameras, anywhere.

"I guess they really want it to be stolen", I smirked.

"I Know right", lily said, I checked all the cameras, there are none in that room".

"Well, did you maybe think there are invisible people lurking in the shadows?

That's when I heard giggles.

"Bingo", I muttered.

CHAPTER 5

It was a giggle, I know very well.

Crap.

Why, did they put only one person on board to watch over the vile, and out of everyone in the whole group, they chose amber?

It's like there screaming for me, to take it?

Yeah, but the thing is, they need to hold their breaths, to keep themselves invisible.

So, she will lose her breath soon.

I turned on the lights and said, "hello, anyone there"?

Then I heard more giggling, "stop, with the giggling".

Its so freaking annoying, "for crying out loud".

Then I heard her say, "I can't let you get the vile".

"How do you know I'm here for the vile"?

"Cause, you're an outcast", she retorted.

"Ok, fair point, you caught me".

"I am here for the vile".

She finally ran out of breath, and was now noticeable.

but the worst part is, she had the audacity, to throw a punch.

I quickly dodged it, touching my necklace to make sure it was on.

The necklace that I just touched, is the thing, that makes my powers stronger.

I got it from my mom.

she was quick in fighting, but i was quicker.

She did a high kick and got me in the noise

"great", i muttered, now my noise is bleeding

She looked at me wide eyed, but all I could do was smirk, wiping the blood from my noise.

Oh, shes gonna wish, she didn't just do that.

As she was distracted, I did a upper cut.

She flew to the ground, coughing at the blow, I just gave her

But, she just had to get back up.

She punched me in the gut, so hard, my stomach felt numb.

"Well, that wasn't very nice", I grunted, trying to breathe out of the lungs, she probably destroyed.

As I gained back my breathing power, I jumped on her, pinning her to the ground.

She tried to get out of my grasp, but I pinned her by the throat. She was coughing for air

But I was not having it.

I used my last remaining strength and punched her.

Right in the gut, I say, that's pretty fair, since she got my gut.

She did a loud groan, I smirked and huffed in her ear "you deserved that one".

I didn't kill her, I just put her in a deep sleep.

That's what I tell myself.

I got up and walked to the vile, put it in my pocket.

I walked over to the window cell and jumped.

thank gosh, I landed on my feet .

I saw lily run- down car, I hopped in and she sped off.

She then asked, "did you get it"?

I smiled, "you bet I did".

I showed her the blue dye in the vile.

"Good", she said, "now throw it out the window".

"hold up, rewind, did you just say throw it out the window"?

"yes", she said.

"I just thought we were gonna use the vile, against the heroes".

"No", lily said, with a chuckle, "we are trying to prevent a war, from breaking out, Skylare".

But, "what about revenge, does that not ring a bell, at all".

"We will get to that later, but in the meantime, I need you to be a spy for us, to see what they are planning".

"Get information, on how they are gonna take us down".

"Got it, then revenge".

"Yes, I muttered

"now, I throw the vile".

I rolled down my window, and threw it.

"well, I hope you are happy".

We finally pulled up into our, little driveway.

Lily and I walked in, I yelled, robs name.

"He's probably downstairs", lily said, tiredly.

I ran downstairs and "I yelled," hey, Rob guess what"?

"What" he said, not looking up from his work, "I got the vile, but, had to sadly destroyed it".

"That's great", he said.

"Oh, and I used my powers".

That's when Rob stopped what he was doing, "you did what," he smiled.

"I used my powers, that my mom and dad gave me".

I showed him my necklace and it was glowing.

He smiled and said, "congratulations Skylare".

"I can't believe you now have your powers".

"Yeah, I said, trying to sound happy".

"What were the side effects", he asked.

While examining me, up and down.

"Well my head was hurting", I said

Ok, he said "how did this happen"?

"Well, I punched her, with super strength".

"Did you kill her"?

"No", I said.

"But, I really wanted to".

"I didn't use my full strength, just knocked her off her feet".

"Good, he said, now, get some rest, you must be tired from all that fighting".

"Actually, I think I could go for another round, don't you think"?

"No, you need to reset your body".

"Ignoring the pain, is not the best for your kind of body".

"So that's a no, on staying up"?

go, to bed, he said.

Well, you're no fun.

I'm not supposed to be.

I rolled my eyes, "goodnight Rob".

I walked back up stairs and said goodnight to lily.

Goodnight, Skylare, sleep tight.

I went to bed happy, cause I used my full powers, for the first time.

I finally, awoken them

The next morning I couldn't wait to see the looks on the council's faces, when they realized the vile is gone.

I brushed my teeth.

and got changed.

I rushed down the stairs and yelled," hurry up lily".

I don't want to be late.

Why so in a rush?, she yawned.

because I just took something of theirs, that they supposedly worked really hard on.

"Well that is a good reason", lily nodded.

"Let me just get grab my purse".

why, "cause I'm going shopping",

"Yeah", but why?

"You don't buy.

"In fact, we don't buy anything, really".

"Yes, but I need something, in the black market".

"What, is it", I said, while walking out of the house.

Um, "it's this new headset", for me.

"It's about time you got a new one".

She rolled her eyes .

I'm just saying, "it's been, what, forever since you changed, the headset".

"Remember that time I almost died, because of your headset".

"It died randomly, and I didn't know how many people, I was going against".

"Yeah, she said," that was scary, wasn't it also your first mission?

"Yeah, it was, indeed, never do that again".

She nodded, "yes, leader" she joked.

I smirked, "don't ever call me that, not yet".

"Yes, leader", she said, teasingly.

"Ha, ha very funny", I said.

"But don't forget, I have the authority, to just kick you out".

"Ok", she said, while pulling into the headquarters.

I got out of the car and I yelled, "Can you please pick me up".

"Yeah, what time"?

"6:00 pm, alright", she said.

Then she drove off.

I walked up the stairs and saw Leo and Conrad, waiting for... me?

"Hey", guys what's up.

"We have some bad news, Conrad said.

"Amber is hurt", he said.

"What", I said, trying not to smile, at the information I just received.

Follow us, we went into the infirmary and saw Mark standing and watching, barely alive amber.

He then mumbled, "who would do such a thing"?

"The outcasts", Scarelett sneered.

"They are the most selfish people to ever walk the earth".

"They don't deserve to be even alive", Scarelett, huffed.

I know what I did was not the best, but I don't feel bad.

She was in my way.

The doctor walked in and said, "she will be fine, just keep her well rested and hydrated".

"The blow really took some of her powers away".

"What do you mean", Leo asked.

Well somehow the person who punched her, went straight for her lungs, and her lungs are very weak".

"And her powers, mostly use her lungs strength".

"We need to keep watch, cause the hit got her good".

"will she be able to still, walk".

"Yes", the doctor, said reassuringly, but just take it slow. We all nodded and the doctor left.

"Wow, how could this even happen".

"Well, Leo said, I read, "the history of the outcasts".

"What do you mean"? Conrad asked,

"I think, the person who almost killed amber, was not a normal outcast", he glanced at me.

"But in fact a leader".

"What, Scarelett said, I thought the leaders were all dead"?

"'Yeah, that's what they want us to think", Conrad chimed.

Leo continued, "the two leaders Lola and Kane, had kids".

Everyone gasped.

I mentally smiled, finally, someone in the heroes group, has a brain.

CHAPTER 6

"How do you know"?

"Well, that's the only way, because there is no one else, who can have powers like that". Leo confirmed.

"Lola, who was very skilled, in combat".

"And Kane, could destroy anything, with just a punch".

"So, you don't think that the prophecy could be coming true",Scarelett asked.

"I am not sure, but, I am certain, that there will be, an uprising", Conrad informed.

suddenly, Amber's eyes, fluttered open.

Her first word was, "I thought I was gonna die".

"How am I, still alive"?, she pondered

"I for sure thought, I was a goner, when i saw, blue.

"What color " Conrad asked.

"Blue, was around her, and her eyes were red".

"That's the same thing that happened to Kane, whenever he was ready for a fight", Conrad muttered.

"But the weird thing is, that she first touched her neck-lace, then she fought me".

"Did you get a glimpse of what the necklace looked like"?, Scarelett pestered.

"It was, gold, and really shiny, that's all i saw".

Yep she is the daughter of Kane and Lola.

Lola has a necklace that doubles her powers.

"Kane has the blue aura around him, and his eyes, looked menancingly at you, before he striked", Conrad grimaced.

"This is crazy", Conrad said, "I have to inform, the coun-cil".

"I agree, this information we got, might start up, another war", Scarelett said.

We left the infirmary, well not all of us, mark stayed.

He said, "he needs to stay with Amber".

We all finally got to the council room.

Conrad said, "let me do the talking, they can be, pretty scary, when they are under a lot of stress".

I don't even know why we are going to them.

The heroes, ignore the problem.

We knocked on the door, and they actually let us in.

Conrad cleared his throat, and said,"we got a problem sir".

Steve sighed, and said, "we already know, we are getting a DNA test done.

Then Conrad asked, "I thought the leaders were power-less".

"Well, we didn't know that they had kids secretly" Steve sighed.

"Well, then, what are we gonna do about this" ?,, Conrad said.

"Well, he said, I don't know , they somehow knew about the vile, before we showed it to the public.

"What, do you think there is a mole"?, Conrad spat out.

"I'm hoping there won't be one, because I can't afford another war".

"Rebuilding, and the people, freaking out, it's just a lot of work", Steve huffed.

"I gotta hand it to you sir", I blurted out," it must really take a toll on you, all the stress."

"Are you mocking me?", he said, while raising a brow, no, sir I'm simply praising you.

"Wait a minute, aren't you the girl who was trying to save one of the outcasts?".

I gritted my teeth, and said, "yes, I believe in justice ,and equality".

"That's nice" he said, "you remind me of Conrad's moth-er, when you said all that".

I felt a hint of disgust, first, getting compared to a hero Just, Ew.

But when i saw Conrad's small smile, I understood he lost someone, he loved dearly.

I gave a comforting smile, to Conrad.

"So, Barbra barked, is amber ok?, Amber is Barbara's only daughter.

"Don't worry, she is in good hands", Conrad reassured her.

"She is awake now".

"Oh thank goodness, i don't know what i would do without her", she said, with a sigh of relief.

"I can't believe that monster just took the vile, like that", Barbra tsked.

"Then on top of that, she might be the daughter of, Lola and Kane".

"I just can't take any more bad news.", Barbra ranted.

Then, karma came.

The door to the council room swung open, a dude holding a swab, said, "well sir, the DNA samples on amber were tested".

"The girl is in fact, the daughter of Lola and Kane.

CHAPTER 7

The room went quiet.

"This can't be", rick said, "they had a daughter?"

"Yes, and, um, she has both her parents powers, combined".

I smiled at that.

Leo gave me look, saying ,what the heck do you know?

"Wow", Steve, "we better go tell the others, about this, we might have to, have a second war".

"Do we really need to go to war, over a little thing, that could easily, be resolved".

He chuckled, and said, "we need to make sure, the outcast know, their place in this society".

Like I said, I never, liked that guy.

Maybe, he is the villian, trying to control, the city.

"you sure there is gonna be a second war", asked rick.

This is gonna be, a disaster, Leo mumbled.

Bring me back to reality.

It's like, he knew, what was up, me personally do, but i would never tell a soul.

Or would I.

We then followed the council, out of the room.

Steve then ordered, that they need to have a meeting, and get to the bottom of this mess.

They made our group sit in the front, so we can really hear the story.

But I know for a fact, they are gonna make up a lie, and cover it up, with more lies, and yadyayda.

I sat down, and I was suddenly shocked, to see Leo, coming over.

He sat next to me.

I then asked, "Do you have a problem with me or something".

"What are you talking about", he sighed.

"Well you ignore me, like the plague, or you're always in a horrible mood.

"I can't read you", he muttered.

"come again", I said, confused.

"Whenever I look at you, I can't see your emotions, at all".

"But when we were at the party, I was nervous".

"Yeah, but that's basic emotion reading, but now, I am confused".

He looked at me, and said, with a sigh, "you are the first person that I can't understand".

"Is that", I smirked.

Yes, it's like there is a sheild, holding me from your feelings.

"Well, I might just be really good at keeping my feelings in the dark".

"What do you think of me", he said quietly.

"I'm not sure, yet?"

"I might never know the real you?"

"But, I will know the fake persona you put on, everyday, I smiled.

"I don't understand that concept, that much", Leo sighed.

"When I was younger, I had this father figure".

"He said, to me, people will judge you on the outside, but you alone, will know the real reason, behind your actions".

"Wow", Leo said, "your father figure was a wise man".

"Yeah, I smirked, he always said the darndest things

"But he died", I said coldly.

How Leo pushed on.

"Let's just say, the world is an unfair place".

"people die, and that's alright, at least he's not suffering like the rest of us".

Leo gave me a small smile, and said, "may he rest in peace".

I nodded, and repeated "may he seriously rest in peace"

Then the fake people, started talking.

I looked straight up, and for the remainder of the time, I didn't look at Leo

Why, did you open up about yourself.

Your supposed to not care about what your fellow collegues think of you.

Rick, then touched the mic, and said" we gathered you here today, to inform you that, someone broke in and stole the vile.

Everyone, in the room started whispering.

"Silence", Rick demanded.

"We did some tests, to see who was the culprit".

"The prophecy is true.

Everyone, then again gasped in amazement.

He continued, and said, "we better keep this confidential for the time being".

Yeah, we don't want your precious statues to have a dent in it do we know, I thought

"The person who broke in, almost took our dear, Amber's life".

"So, we better take her down", Rick said, while narrowing his eyes.

Impressive, they didn't lie this time, that's a first.

"Now, we need to find this girl , cause this girl, is the daughter of our worst enemies".

"She is the daughter of, Lola and Kane".

The room went silent.

Rick then continued, "she has both her parents powers, combined".

"So, we better keep on our toes, cause with just one hit, you will be, legally dead".

"Now, I am asking for volunteers to work on this case?"

The room went silent, again.

Rick scanned the room.

He then, looked at Conrad, and said, "how about the soul group work on this case".

Since, it affected you, the most, I think it's best if you guys take the case.

Of course, he's using the guild card, what an original guy, he truly is.

Conrad nodded, and said, "yes sir".

"Great", Rick smiled, he cleared his throat, and said, "you all may be excused".

My group was about to leave, when Rick stopped us, and said," he needed us to come back tomorrow extra early".

"Cause you guys need to train, train, train",.

Everyone was definitely groaning, mentally.

But physically, we were smiling and nodding.

Conrad then leaned in and whispered, "welcome to my world, he smiled".

I smiled, and said,"Sucks to me you, huh".

Then the devil came, "what are you two laughing about", Scarelett asked.

I rolled my eyes, and said, "nothing to get your two faced head wrapped around".

She gaped at me.

I smiled, and said, "I should actually get going, I have a date".

I walked away leaving them in shock.

Why, did I say that, we all know that, I could never pull a guy.

I walked out, as I was walking down the stairs, Leo, came out of nowhere.

He asked If I was busy.

I declined, but he said why, not.

I have plans, I said bluntly.

"What are your plans", he asked, while, giving me an up and down.

"I have a dog to take care of, it has fleas".

What a freaking lie.

"And my house, it's a mess, and I have chores, and other stuff".

He smirked and leaned down to my ear, "you know, you don't have to lie about it"

My face turned red, I really didn't, but why, did I?

"Well, I said awkwardly I got to go, my sis is waiting for me".

As I walked away, I could feel him try to read my emotions, but I wouldn't let him.

I knew, I needed to keep my distance, from Leo.

I saw lily, sitting in the car, eating a bag of potato chips.

I opened up the door and plopped in.

"So" ,she said, buckling up," how was your day".

"The council was pretty mad", I smiled.

"Yeah," lily smirked.

"Also, they made my group, the ones to find me, funny, huh?

Lily smirked, and said, "what a bunch of dense people".

"I know, right".

"So, has anyone suspected your powers, yet?"

"Nope, they think nothing of it".

"Except, for this one guy".

"Oh, no," lily groaned, "what did you do?"

"It's not what I did", I said defensively.

"I sorta opened up", and he said, "how he can't read my emotions, which I was confused".

"He also knows the story of my mom and dad, how they had children, and he kept glancing at me"?

"That's weird?", she said.

"Well duh", it should be.

"What should I do?"

"Whatever you do, don't, distance yourself".

"He will think something is up, if you do".

""What's his last name?," "I'm not sure?", he didn't say.

"Well,she said" you do know, he could be with the other group".

"What do you mean," other group?

"Well", she said," "long ago, there were actually, three groups of outcasters".

"Your parents groups and others".

"What is the other?"

"Well, that's the problem, they didn't hate the heroes, as much as the outcast did".

"They also, didn't fight in the war with us".

"Do you think Leo is part of the unknown group?"

"They have a name, ok. What's there name.

Well, they are called, the mind readers".

"But we call them,the deadly sirens".

"So,you think Leo has the emotional powers, that's like mind reading, but just different".

"Yes, and since we are on the topic of the mindreader, they also invited all the leaders to a gathering".

"What", I said, "you're joking".

"Nope, true facts, since you are now open of being a leader, you are not permitted to go to the gatherings"

"And your brother will be there".

I sighed, and thought its been awhile.

CHAPTER 8

We got back to my house, I laid on the couch, and sighed.

What a day.

But that was quickly taken away, when lily, said, "you should probably get ready".

"What's wrong with my outfit?"

"You need to look your best, and besides, what you're wearing, isn't giving, leader vibes".

"Judgey much," I muttered

I sighed, and said, "When is the gathering?"

"like, in ten minutes", she smiled.

"Dude", I said," why didn't you tell me, I had ten minutes".

She shrugged, short term memory loss?"

I rolled my eyes, went up from the couch, and slammed my bedroom.

I picked out an outfit that flashed, leader vibes.

I checked in my full length mirror, and said, "you got this".

Lily, yelled, "hurry up".

I sighed, and said, "coming".

"Ok, lets go", I smiled.

"Aren't you forgetting something, or should I say someone", a voice said, behind me.

"Omy gosh, almost forgot about Rob".

He growled, and said, "very funny girls".

We all got in the rundown car.

lily says, it runs like a new one.

Note to self, bring lily to an eye doctor.

Her eyes kinda giving, blind girl vibes, when she is driving, on the road.

The car ride only took, fifteen minutes.

We finally got there, and hopped, out of the car.

there were two guys standing out, and they said, "who are you?"

I'm, Skylare walker, and these are my helpers.

They gave me an up and down look.

Then, one guard whispered in the other guy's ear.

"Alright, you may come in".

I walked in and we sat down, at our assigned tables.

I asked, lily "if the group leader from the mind reader had a son".

She nodded, and said, "I think they do, he's also around, your age".

"What is his name?"

"I think it's, Leo".

"Why, are you asking?"

"Hold up, isn't that the guy, you were talking about earlier?"

I nodded, and said, "yes it was".

The thing finally began, and the mind readers came around to each group, saying their, "hello's".

I tried to slouch down, so they didn't have to see me.

But when the leader came up to my table, asking, "who is the so-called new leader".

I slumped up and said, "I am".

He tried to give me an up and down, but I stopped him, asking, "if there was a problem".

"No", he said, "my son, was talking to me a little bit ago, about a girl, he met".

"That might be the one who will save us all".

"I thought , he was talking gibberish".

"Well, I am the daughter of Lola and Kane".

"yes", he said, I heard of the prophecies, and stuff.

"So, I said, is your son coming tonight?"

"Um, yes," he said, "he might be a little bit late".

"Cause he just is very busy".

"What does he do?"

"Well my son, is going undercover as a hero in training, at the headquarters, W.C.H."

"He's been doing it for like, his whole life".

I made a nervous smile, and said, "that's funny, cause I met this guy, who is um, very quiet interesting".

"Really", the mind reader said.

"Yeah, I think his name was, Leo".

" isn't that funny, cause my son's name, is Leo".

Then I heard a familiar voice, behind me, saying, "I'm here, father".

I think you might, know someone here, "son".

Then, when I turned my head, ,Leo was glaring at me.

"What, cat got your tongue?"

Leo, did a sigh, "father, can I talk to Skylare, or whatever her name is".

"Yes, and everyone at the table, my leave", Leo ordered.

As they left, Leo, narrowed his eyes, and said, "what are you doing here?"

"Hello, to you".

"Stop messing, with me, what are you doing here?"

"Well, I am the leader, of the outcast", I retorted.

"What, he said, is impossible".

"Well, I am the daughter, of Lola and Kane".

Then he put two and two together.

"No, way he said, I knew it".

"What do you mean, you knew it?"

"I knew you were the daughter", he smirked.

"The first day, when you came in, I knew something was off".

"How?", I asked.

"Well, I couldn't sense your emotions, and you were just, different".

"And how you mouthed sorry, to a villian".

"So", I said, "are you like, the new leader, in the mind readers group?"

"Soon", he sighed heavily.

"Why, don't you sound so happy about it?"

"I am",he said, "I'm just worried, that I won't do a good job".

"Well, you think your job is hard, I'm the leader, of the whole sha-bang".

"I am only, fifteen".

"Yeah", he said, with a smile, "I shouldn't get to worked up, should I?"

"So, were you impressed, that I actually stole the vile?"

"Sorta", he said, " I was shocked, mostly".

"Wait", he said, "what's your real name?"

"What do you mean, real name?"

He rolled his eyes, and said, "stop playing with me, and just answer the question".

"My name is, Skylar walker", I smiled.

He choked on his water, and he said, "what really?"

"You, ok?"

"I'm fine", he said.

"So", the mind reader said, "how are you two youngsters doing?"

"Good", I smirked, "alright", I said, seriously.

"I'm gonna make this quick and easy".

The mind reader raised his eyebrow, at my question.

"I want your son, to help me take down the heroes"

"Leo, looked at me, and I smirked.

He then muttered, "I'm not a pro, like Skylare".

"I can teach you", I smiled.

"No", he said giving me the side eye.

"what would it hurt your ego?", I mocked

He groaned, and said, "dad I'm leaving".

He then stormed away

"Well, that's was, dramatic", I mumbled.

"I'm sorry about that, the leader smiled, he is not used to girls being above him".

"Yeah", I said, I understand.

"I hope you don't hate him for his short temper", the mind reader said.

I shook my head and said, "he's fine".

"Oh", the headmaster smiled, "why don't you and Leo get together?".

"No", I said, annoyed

"Why, you already got someone?"

"No, I frankly don't think, me and your son will be good partners".

"I'm just saying, when you get kids, you got to choose, what group, you want your kids to have"

"But, I don't think I need to get married, right now".

"I'm only fifteen".

"No", he said, looking into my eyes, is he really trying to, "manipulate me"

what a turd.

I leaned in, and said, "no, you cant, I blocked"

He chuckled ,and said, "you truly are the daughter, of Lola and Kane."

Then I heard a voice behind me.

"Hey, Skylare how are you?"

Oh brother, I muttered.

CHAPTER 9

I felt so much force, from the back hug, he gave me.

" I haven't seen you in, how many years".

Then my eye caught a girl, behind him.

"Who's she?", I asked

"My fiance", he smiled.

"What group is she from?"

"Your's" he said, hesitantly.

"What", I said, "you took one of my people, without asking?"

"Dang, mike, how I want to, - ugg.

"You know what ,I'm just mad, you didn't tell me, you were getting married".

"Sorry", he said, "but guess what, I heard, you got your powers".

"Yeah, I did".

"So, what parent power, did you get?"

"Both", I smirked.

"Both" he repeated, while in shock.

"So, you're the one, I have to bow down to?"

"Yes", I said, with a smile, "I'm the one, who will save, our people".

"Oh yeah, I forgot your the leader of me too.

"Yeah, isn't this the best day ever".

"for you, it, is, anyways, Sofia is um, tired, so we are gonna go, sit down".

As he was leaving, I saw a glimpse of Sofia.

Wow, I thought shes really, pretty.

Short blonde hair, and blue eyes.

"See", the mind reader said, "your brother is married".

"Ok, that's it, I am gonna go all ham on this dude, if he doesn't just, shut up".

"Shut up" I said, but when I waved my hands, blue smoke flames came out.

The mind reader flew backwards, landing on his butt.

Everyone, stopped, and stared at me.

Rob and Lily, got up and saw what I just did, rushing over, to my aid.

Lily helped the mind reader up, and Rob, was, well rob.

We left,after that whole thing, "It could have gone worse", lily reassured.

"Yeah, at least I didn't kill him, that would have been bad".

"Yeah, you would have been a goner, for sure", Rob said.

"Thanks, Rob, I really needed that".

"Hey, lily can you drop me off, at the park".

"Why", lily sighed.

"Cause, I have some business, to take care of".

She turned, to go to the playground.

She parked, and I got out.

She rolled down her window, saying, "should I wait?"

"No", I said, "just go, I will be home later tonight, don't, wait up".

She nodded, and I walked into the park.

I saw a figure, it was Leo.

"What are you doing here"? he said, not even, looking back.

"I thought, I would keep you, some company, lonely boy".

"I thought, you were busy?", he asked

"Not anymore, I'm not", I said.

"I went to the most pointless meeting, of my life".

"And, I don't even know why people want you and me to get married, or end up together?"

"Really?", he smirked.

I sighed, and said, "that's why you left early?"

"I thought, at first It was something that I said, or did, that made you feel, uncomfortable?"

"Yeah, it was sorta, kinda, your present".

"Oh, Is that so, then, I should go then?"

I was about to fake leave, when he grabbed my wrist, and sat me down.

"Well", I said, "your dad might hate me, now".

"What, did you do?"

"Well, he was really getting on my last nerve, so I used, my powers on him".

"Is he ok?", Leo said blankly.

"Yeah, but I got kicked out of the party for sure".

He chuckled.

I raised my eyebrow, and asked, "is that funny to you?"

"Yes", he said, giving me the eyes.

"Well",I said, "I should go its getting pretty cold".

"No", he said, "don't go".

I smirked, and said, "what was that, I couldn't hear you?"

he grunted, and said, "please, don't make me repeat it"

I shrugged, and said, "fine i won't but next time, use your words"

I sat back down, in silence.

Till, I said, "why do you come at night?"

"Well", he said, while looking out, "my mom, would take me, when I was younger".

"Is this the same bench, she would sit in?"

"Yes", he said.

"What was your moms name?"

"Sarah", he said.

"Oh, wasn't she the leader, with your dad?"

"Yeah, lily told me, she was the sweetest person to ever be an outcast".

"Yeah", he said sadly.

"You alright?", I asked.

He shook his head and said, "I'm fine, I just like my quiet".

I was quiet, for like two whole minutes, when I couldn't take it anymore.

"How can you sit here, and not say a word?"

"Well", he said, "I just practice".

"How do you practice being quiet?"

"First, you close your mouth, then here comes the hard part, so pay attention, you sit and don't talk", he mocked.

"I get it", I muttered.

We sat again, in silence, just enjoying, the night sky.

"I'm kinda cold", I complained.

He then got closer to me.

I also got closer.

He then said, "I'm doing this, so you don't complain, alright, don't get any ideas".

I smirked, and said, "whatever makes you sleep at night Leo".

"Thanks", I said while snuggling up to him.

"You cold anymore?", he asked.

"Not too cold really", I said.

"But, did you really have to choose the coldest nights, to go star watching?"

He shrugs, and said, "the cold never bothers me really".

What a true, Elsa guy, he is.

Also he smelled to die for.

Note to self, ask where he got the cologne.

"Are you smelling me", Leo asked.

"Yes", I said, "it suits you well".

"Thank you, for smelling me?"

"Hey, I know you don't like talking about her, but how did she die?"

"She went to war, just like everyone else", Leo said.

"Wait, but your mom is a mind-reader?"

"What", he said, "what's so wrong about them" he said, defensively.

"Nothing's wrong with that, I just thought, they weren't part of the outcast really?"

"Well, my mom, was married into the mind readers, she wasn't actually one."

"Her skills were amazing, everyone wanted to be her", Leo smiled.

"But when the war happened, everyone assumed she was dead", he tensed.

"Because, that was what happened, to every other main leader".

"Well", I said, "there might be a chance, she might be alive?"

"No", he said, while shaking his head.

"Why, not she could be alive".

"No, I already tried to find her", he said quietly

"What", I said, "you already tried to look for her?"

"Yes, I already told you, so can we stop talking about it".

I nodded, and said, "fine".

We sat in silence and snuggled closer, into his shoulder.

He tensed up a little.

I rolled my eyes, and muttered, "Leo, stop, tensing up, I wont bite".

He listened, and I closed my eyes.

Giving me the best sleep, I had in a very long time.

CHAPTER 10

T he next morning I woke up, alone.

Leo was gone, and I was alone.

I checked my phone, lily was trying to get a hold of me.

"Crap", I groaned.

I got up, and I said to myself, why can't you trust anyone to stay, or even have the decency to wake a girl up.

I called lily, and she quickly, picked up.

She started screaming, saying, "what on earth Skylare".

I groaned, again, saying, "it's too early for yelling, can you just pick me up".

"You're still at the park", lily asked.

I hummed, a yes.

"Alright I'll be there soon", lily told.

A couple minutes later, lily pulled up, looking madder, than ever.

I hopped in, and said, "can you just take me to Leo's place".

"I gotta have a little chat, with him".

We headed to Leo's, in silence.

Leo's house was huge, that the president, was probably, jealous.

I got out, and said, "I'll call you".

lily, gritted her teeth, and said, "that's what you said last time".

"Oh, I'm positive", I said, while cracking, my muscles.

She left, without saying, goodbye.

I rang the doorbell, and a maid came, and she said, "what do you want?", in a not so cheery voice.

"I need to talk to Leo", I asked.

"Oh, master Leo is busy at the moment", she tisked.

She was about to close the door.

"Wait",I said, trying to stop her, from shutting the door.

She sighed, and said, "you must be, Skylare walker, huh".

I nodded, and said, "you heard of me".

She nodded.

"It's important", I pleaded.

She rolled her eyes, and said,"his way to master, Leo".

I walked into their house, and sheesh, they got the whole shabang, in there.

She took me outside, where she said, "he is with his trainer, so be quiet".

I nodded, and she left.

I heard, men grunting, Leo was fighting well, woah, he's a good fighter.

The trainer was the one yelling at Leo.

"Hey", I said, while walking towards them.

Leo, and I the trainer were alarmed.

Leo, gave me the glare and I said, "what's up Leo, we need to talk?"

"Who's this?", the trainer, said.

"Nobody", Leo huffed.

"Ouch"I said, "hi I'm Skylare".

"Hi, Skylare, do you mind sitting somewhere, so we can finish the training?"

I walked over and sat on the beach, reminding me of last night.

I saw Leo fighting , his stances were good, his movement was breathe taking.

He finally was done with his training.

The trainer, bowed and said good job, master Leo.

Leo, nodded and the trainer left, Leo, stood there huffing and puffing.

I got up, and said, "what's with all this master, crap".

He chuckled, and said, "its my dad's house".

"He is a rich guy".

"Who, sells illegal crap, that the heroes, don't know about".

"Bingo", Leo smirked.

"Well, you look like a person, that would be called, master".

"Thanks?", he said.

"No, problem", I smirked.

"Why, are you here, anyways?", Leo asked.

"Well, I just wanted to see how you were doing".

"Oh no", he said, "what did I do?"

"Nothing", I said, "just have a quick question to ask".

He groaned, and said, "its to early for your rambling, skylare".

"No, its a good one, why didn't you wake me up.

"What do you mean?"

"Let me jog, your short term memory, you, me, park, last night, I fell asleep".

"Oh", he said, "I am so sorry, I totally forgot about you".

"Alright", I said, "I forgive you, just don't do it again".

"Who," said there was gonna be a next time?"

"I said that, I'm sorry but, that was the longest sleep, I had, in a long time.

"I want to do it again, tonight".

"How about, we have a s'mores party, why don't I invite my friends, from my group.

"And we can all, star gaze night?"

"Sounds perfect", I said.

"So", I said, "your training, huh".

"Gotta be the best", he smirked.

"Well", I said, "if you want my opinion, which I know you don't, but I don't care".

"Stand in the position you know you like".

He did, and said, "that's good, but I think you need to be more comfortable".

I touched his elbow, wanting to angled it better.

"What are you doing?" he said, still standing in the pose.

"your pose is fine", I smiled

"But you need to focus, you look distracted?"

"No, I'm fine",he tried to reassure himself

"I'm not meaning physical, but mentally".

He let go of the pose and he said, again, "I'm fine".

"Alright", I said, "but if you want to be the best, you need to have a clear mind on the battlefield".

I sat next to him.

"I know", he said," I just don't know what's gone over me".

" I just don't feel like myself, personally", he sighed.

" When did this start"?

"Yesterday, when I realized you were, Skylares".

"Oh", I said," well, why, is that troubling you?"

"I don't know" he said, getting a little bit annoyed.

"Sorry", I said.

"Just trying to be a supportive friend".

He looked at me oddly.

"We are not friends?", he huffed

"What", I said, kinda hurt, at his words.

"We are not friends, we're supposed to be enemies".

"No, we are supposed to take down the heroes together, I reassured him.

There is no, "we" either, he scoffed.

"What", I said, "what do you mean, you can't be near me?"

"Your powers affect my powers".

"I can't use my powers, the way I am supposed to, because of you".

"So, you staying, I make you nervous".

"Yes", he said," now you get it".

"I think you have a crush on me?", I smiled.

"Me, having a crush on you, no, I would never, you are not my type, I could never date a girl like you".

"What's so wrong about a girl like me?"

"Cause", he said, trying to make a good sense of what he wants to say

"Well", I said, "whats your answer gonna be?"

"Oh, wait, you have none".

"But, I think me and you would be perfect together", I smirked.

"What", he said, blushing a little.

"See, I make you blush, that must be a sign".

"Just go", he said, trying to cover up his smile.

"Ok" I said ,getting up and leaving, "see you tonight".

I sat outside on the steps, and called, lily.

She picked me up, and she said, "how did it go?"

I smiled, and said, "it went very good".

"that's good", lily nodded.

"Oh, we also need to meet someone".

"Who?", she said.

"Phin, he would know".

"Oh, no, lily said, "why phin?"

"Cause, he is the only one, who can answer my question"

"Now, step on the gas, old lady".

She sped up, taking me to the swamp.

Cause, he is a non-social person.

I got out of the car, and knocked on the wooden door.

He yelled, in his annoyed voice, "I don't want your high, in sugar, cookies".

"It's skylare", I yelled back.

I heard some rummaging, then the door, flung open.

"Hi", he said, in a very, happy voice.

"Hey, are you busy?"

"No", he said, "just redoing the library".

"Ok, good:, I walked in.

Phin, is like an older brother to me, even though I have one.

He filled in his place ,when he was gone, as the leader of my mothers group.

He is only two years older, not much, but he is like the smartest person in the city.

"Hey, phin, I have a question, I want you to answer".

"Hit me with it", he smirked, while sitting down.

"Ok", I said, "do you know why the mind readers want me and Leo together?"

He thought for a moment, "well the prophecy did change".

"What do you mean by change?"

"Well, the mind readers group, they are always suspicious of the destruction and the combat group".

"Why's that?"

"Well", he said, "the mind readers think, it's unfair, that their kids don't easily get a chance to show off their skill, to Fana".

"Who's she?"

"Well, she is the one who can change the fate for the people, of the outcasts".

"She chose you, as the leader of the outcast, and realm".

"Oh, nice".

"Why, didn't the mind readers get a chance?"

"No, one knows, skylare, and no one, will ask"

"Why", I said, he shrugged, "I don't even know, and for a guy who knows a lot, its pretty scary"

"Maybe the council will help?", phin said

I nodded, "well should I be worried, about the mind readers?"

"I don't know", he said, "they are still one of us, just don't trust them too much".

"I see", I said, "well look at the time".

"Where are you off to?", phin smirked.

"I have to go to the house of the guy, that "doesn't like me".

"Great", he said, "have fun and be careful".

I left his house, and I said, to lily, while getting in the car, "drop me off at home.

She sniffed and said, "you gonna take a shower to?"

"I'm just saying, you kinda smell like swamp".

We got home, and I took a shower, and said to lily, "what should I wear?"

Lily walked in my closet, and picked out this outfit.

"cute", I smiled

"I know, Leo is gonna be swooning", lily joked.

I rolled my eyes and said, "lets just get going".

We got in the car again, and I said, to lily, "i'll call, you when i am done".

She smiled, "have fun".

"But not too much fun, and the gross part was, she winked.

I yelled back, "don't make it weird".

CHAPTER 11

I ran the doorbell, and the maid from earlier, answered.

she sighed, and said, "Leos in the back".

I smiled, and said, "thanks".

She took me to him, again, When she left I had a thought, I'ma creep up on him.

But, before I could, he said, "what do you want?"

"Dang your good",I smirked.

"Why, are you here so early?", he said, confused

"I thought I could, help out".

"Why, would you do that?", he huffed.

"Because, I'm a nice person, and I can, if I want to".

"Why, are you being so nice to me, is what I wanted to say".

"Because, the prophecy said, that we're gonna work, together".

I stepped closer to him, but he backed away.

"There is again, no, us, and you know that, so get over it".

"Fine", I said, while sitting down, on the bench.

"I brought a blanket, so me and you could sit together, as companions".

"Over even more", I smirked.

He rolled his eyes, and said, "fine we can sit with each other".

"Also, did you know we have a council?"

"Yeah", he said, "I know that, everyone should know that".

Well, I didn't I muttered.

"Well", he said, while sitting down, I heard that they changed the prophecy, like a million times".

"They did?," I said, leaning in.

"No", he said, "your way to gullible".

I'm sorry" I said, while giving him the puppy eyes.

"Don't do that", he said, looking away, "I don't like it".

"Oh, sorry:", I said, again.

"Don't be", he said.

We then sat in silence and I randomly asked," got a girlfriend?"

"No", he said, quickly.

"Oh", I said, a little bit excited.

"why did you ask?", he smirked

"Well, if we ever be more than friends, I don want to be still hungover on your ex", I smiled

"What, you think, that me and you, would be more, than you know?"

"No, I don't know, what you mean?", I smirked

"Well we are humans, that are close, but aren't close, then we must be enemies", I sighed.

"No", he said, "I don't hate you".

"Ah, I'm honored, I said, while touching my heart.

He rolled his eyes, "who did you invite?"

"No one", I mumbled, "I don't really have many friends".

"Shocker", he said.

"Ouch, that kinda hurt", I gasped.

"What," he said .

"The reason I don't have friends is because, I'm busy, but at the same time, I don't really need friends, to keep me going.

"But you want someone at the same time?" Leo asked.

"Yes, exactly, I don't care, but at the same time I want friends".

"Well" he said, tonight you are gonna meet more people", he reassured.

Then a butler came , and said, "master, your friends, are here".

"Bring them in", he said.

"Will do sir", the butler bowed.

It wasn't a lot of people, but just the right amount.

Three boys, and two girls, were there.

Leo got up from his seat ,and said, "welcome guys".

The boys did a bro thing, and the girls smiled, and said, "how, do you do".

I felt somewhat weird around all these upper class, weirdos.

Then he finally, introduced me, and they said, "hi, but except for one".

She just looked mad.

"So, you're the one who hurt my uncle?", she sneered

"What are you talking about?", I said, innocently

"Well, let me tell you, I don't think you are cut out for being the so called chosen one".

"It should have been Leo, but no they had to pick you".

"I'm sorry, did you not get your way?", I sighed

"Well,tough nails, life is not fair, so get over it".

She scoffed, "you little"- "enough", Leo interjected.

Cousin, I don't like people disrespecting the mind readers like that".

"Rose, wasn't it, I wouldn't do anything, you might regret".

"Then she had the ballz to say, "why are you even here".

I titled my head and said, "because I am watching the starts, with your cousin".

"That's fine with you right?"

I could tell my plan was working, when I saw Leo blush, so much for not being friends.

"Bro, I can't believe you", Matt said.

"If you aren't anything, then why are you guys standing so close to each other?", Matt scoffed.

"Because she is cold", Leo lied.

"Yeah", I said, "its none of your dang business", I retorted.

Mat shook his head, and said, not cool dude".

"Omygosh" I said, while switching my eye color, to red, and my blue aura around me.

"Me and Leo, are not a thing, I angrily

They all nodded, and Leo, well he, was unfazed by what I did.

Which didn't shock me, cause his dad is the mind reader, himself.

"Well" I said, going back to normal, " Shall we go by the fire and do s'mores?"

Everyone said yes, and I said, "good, now lets go".

We all sat down around the fire pit .

No, one wanted to say a word, because of what just happened.

"So", I said, "I want to get to know you all"

"How about, we go around and say, "what are powers are, and are names?", I asked

"Ok, now, I will go first, I'm skylare, and my powers are very skilled in combat".

I also, I   can destroy with just a touch, so I would keep that one in mind", I said, with a sweet face.

"Now, your turn Leo".

Well he said, "everyone, here already knows my name?", he rolled his eyes.

I sighed and said, "Just do it for me".

"OK", he said, "I'm Leo, and my powers are emotional reading, I can sense if someone is lying"

"Cool", I said, "now, who wants to go next?"

I turned to rose, but she said, "I'm not doing this first grader, get to know you game."

I gave her the red eyes, and she quickly changed her answer.

"Well", she said I'm rose, and my power is that I can manipulate anyone, with the sound of my soothe voice".

"so like a siren?", I asked

"No", she said, "everyone keeps mistaking that, we are mind readers, not sirens".

"I'm sorry, have you ever used it?"

"No", she said, "I just got it".

"Oh", I said, well who's next, then?"

"Me, someone"said, "It's my turn".

"Great", I said, "what's your name?"

"My name, is Lucy, and my power is to make people fall in love".

"What", I said, "how do you do that?"

"Well, just with some focus and I can just make anyone swoon over me.

"But it only lasts an hour", Lucy said.

"sweet", I said, "next?"

I guy raised his hand, and said, "I'm mat, and my power is , I destroy peoples Minds".

"That's, interesting, I've never heard of that, before?"

"Ok , anyone else that I forgot?",

I heard a girls voice, saying, "I'm the last one" she smiled.

"Well I'm crystal, and my power is, I can calms one mind, with just the sound of my voice"

"Cute", I said.

She smiled and said, "I never thought, you, would be so nice?".

"What do you mean, so nice?"

"Well, the mind reader said, that you are the hardest person to talk to, about serous matters".

"And that it should have been Leo, being the chosen one".

" I see, but Leo isn't the leader of the whole shabang, and I think you, all need to get used to that", I said.

"Not everything you work for, will benefit you", I said wisely

They all looked at me, like I was speaking a foreign tongue.

"Well", Leo said, "I didn't know, you could be so wise?"

"Me either?" I said, "I too, scared myself".

"well isn't it Skylare walker, in the flesh", a deep but soft, males voice said.

I turned my head, "who said that?", I looked around, then I spotted a figure.

"Well, let me properly introduce myself, I'm Lucas, I'm Leo's brother".

CHAPTER 12

"You had a brother, and you didn't tell me?", I glared, at Leo.

He shrugged, and said, "you never" asked.

"Also, we don't talk much, alright".

"What are you doing here?", Leo said annoyed

"What's wrong brother, I can't be in my own house, any-more?"

"Well, i wouldn't say your house",Leo scoffed.

"Oh, come on brother, me and you, were so close", Lucas smirked

"Not anymore we aren't", Leo said, displeased.

"he sighed and said, "just tell me, why, you are here?"

"I want to see Skylare", he said bluntly

"People have been talking about her, and i wanted to see, if the rumors, are true", Lucas said.

"Ok, when are you leaving, because dad will get mad, seeing your face" Leo said coldy.

"I'm not staying with you", Lucas smirked

"I wanted to ask, if i could stay with Skylare", he turned to face me.

I was confused, about what he just said.

"You rather stay at my crappy place then here, I scoffed.

"Well on the behalf of the council", Lucas reassured.

"Wait, you know the council?", I smiled

Lucas nodded, and said, "I help them out, time to time".

I nodded and said, "that's great".

Leo, rolled his eyes, but i glared at him.

He ignored it, what a turd I thought.

"well" I said," if you excuse me, we're gonna to star gazing".

I took Leo's hand and he started to blush at the action.

I laid out the blanket, and we sat down.

"I can't believe you have a brother, and you didn't tell me?"

"He is not, my brother", Leo huffed.

"Oh, come on, he is your brother", I sighed.

"No, we aren't", Leo scoffed.

"You already said that?", I smiled.

"Well", he said, "I hate that man, he does not deserve to be called family, or brother".

"Wow, wow, wow, slow your role buster, you and Lucas ,are family".

"Families, are supposed to have each other's back, ok", I argued.

"If you knew him, and his true intentions, you would understand", Leo sneered.

"Now, stop talking, and look at the stares", Leo barked.

I did as i was told, in the corner of my eye, I could see Lucas, looking at me and Leo, from afar.

I thought, it was smart, to let Lucas stay with me.

What if Leo is right, what if he is trying to ruin everything, and doesn't really care?"

Well, I guess I have to go back to phin's place, to get my answer.

The star gazing was finally over, I walked up to lucas and said, "lily will be picking us up".

He smiled, and said, "thank you for letting me stay, with you."

"No problem",I smiled.

Then Leo came from behind, and whispered in my ear, saying, "I'm taking you to the headquarters tomorrow".

When he was finished, he side-eyed Lucas, as he passed by him.

Boys, and I right?

"What was that all about?", Lucas, asked.

Leo asked if he could pick me up and I said yes.

"Interesting", Lucas smirked.

"Anyways, lily might be here, we should go, and check".

We walked out, and Lilys run down car, was waiting for us.

I told lily, that Lucas, will be staying with us, for the time being.

"Thee, Lucas", she gasped.

"Yeah", I said, "what's so cool about the guy, he just works for the council"? I said, while slamming the door shut.

" Lucas, is not just a guy, he is the first mind-reader to be part of the council", lily smiled.

"No way", I said, "that's why Leo doesn't l"ike you?"

"Skylare", lily groaned "manners, do exist".

"No worries, Lucas chuckled, "I'm used to it".

"I did go behind my family's back, and went to the realm, to follow my dreams", he confessed.

"That's amazing, you followed your dreams", I reassured him.

"Yeah", he said, "I just thought my family would support it to?", he sighed

The rest of the car ride was in a comfortable, silence.

We finally got home, and I said, to Lucas, "the guest room is just around that corner".

I have so many questions, I wanted him to answer, and so many things, I wanted to happen, or change.

But life's not like that, sadly, I mean, I need to get over it.

I woke up the next morning, with very little sleep.

I brushed my teeth and got changed, did a quick fit check, and left.

I walked out, seeing Lucas, already up and making coffee.

"Good morning", he said.

"Good morning", I grumbled.

"You alright?", he smirked, "you look sickly".

"I didn't get much sleep, too much on my mind", I sighed.

"Same, I get these nightmares, about", he paused

"What?" I said, curiosity.

"Nothing", he said, while taking a sip of his coffee.

Oh, I hope he burns the roof of his mouth, on that coffee, now.

Suddenly, I heard a knock, "that must be Leo", I sighed.

I opened up a the door and there he was he.

He was wearing, denim jeans and a black t-shirt.

"You look nice", I smiled.

"You, ready", he said, ignoring my compliments, I see.

I walked to his car and I said, to him, "what would you do if you were still the chosen one?"

"Well", he said, "I would first go to the council, and ask for."

He thought for a moment, "never mind", he said.

"What," I said, "you can't leave me hanging, what did you want to ask the council?"

"You will understand later, ok so just don't worry", Leo said

"Oh don't worry, I'm gonna worry my little head off", I screeched

Whatever don't tell me I don't even want to know I will just find out.

We got out of his car and we were now walking up the stairs.

"Ok' he said, "today we will be", but I cut him off saying, "Yadadda, I don't care, I groaned.

"Why, are you being like this?", Leo asked.

"Well, cause I can", and I walked away.

He followed me, and said, "oh come on Skylare".

I turned around, not realizing , we were close.

"My name, is not Skylare, it's sky, alright" I said, coldly.

"You're lucky we are in a public place, or would of kick you in the ballz", I smirked.

He gulped, and said, "got it". .

We walked over, and Conrad turned to us and said, "guess what guys, its official".

"We are on the case, on catching the daughter of, Lola and Kane".

"Anyways, the council wants us to look over these files".

"So, I thought, why don't we eat, and work?"

"What I'm trying to say is we were going out for brunch", Conrad smiled, brightly.

"Good, I forgot to eat breakfast, also I'm a food girly, so don't mind me, pounding on a pancake".

"Perfect," Conrad smiled.

CHAPTER 13

Conrad drove us to lilies brunch inn.

We all sat down, mark sat across from amber, Conrad and scarlett sat across from each other, so did me and Leo.

"Ok guys, we got some intel about the women in the mask.

"Them women in the mast i smirked, "what a nice name.

Leo, kicked me under the chair. We know that she is part of the destruction group, Conrad continues.

"But she also has the powers of combat", scarelett added.

"Yes, your right", Conrad nodded.

"But how are we gonna locate her?", i asked.

"That's the tricky part", Conrad informed.

"But we did locate, the vile, amber said.

"It looks like in these pics, the mask women just dropped it", Conrad pointed out.

"Well, then why are we looking for her, if she doesn't have the vile?".

"She comited a serious crime", Scarelett sneered.

"The vile the only thing we could use, to take down the outcast?", Amber sighed.

"Wait so you're telling me, the outcast could take us down?".

"Yes", Conrad said.

"But we just keep them on a short leash, you know so they don't cross the line", Scareletts smirked.

I tried not to smile, but I felt angry.

"Why are we even fighting with the outcast, if they could just kill us?", I asked.

"Well, Conrad said its complicated".

I rolled my eyes everything is complicated.

"well, how are we gonna find this woman?", Scarelett huffed.

"Well I did have an idea but it's absurd", I said, quietly.

"Oh then, lets not hear about it, Scarelett said, annoyed.

Conrad nodded for me to continue.

"Well, my father said to me, that the villian's are gonna make war, so I was thinking, what if we try to make peace?".

"What kind of plan is that?", is that Scarelett sneered.

"yeah", Amber said, they tried to kill me.

"But the thing I don't understand is, that she didn't kill me"?, amber pondered.

" What I see is a advantage, Conrad smiled.

"What do you mean", I asked.

"Well the reason that they must not kill, is because of the war".

"Why was there even a war?", I asked.

"Don't worry about it", Conrad said, it was a day where a lot of lives, were list, and death was all around".

"I see, well what started the war anyways?", I asked.

"Oh you don't know the history of the war?", Conrad asked.

"Not really, I shrugged.

"Well some say Lola was a hero slash villian".

"What do you mean, hero, slash villian?, I asked.

Lola used to work in the field, Scarelett added.

"She was super smart", Amber said.

"But she did some digging in the files, and she found a way, to make made own powers", Conrad said, while shaking his head.

"What", I said she made her own powers, ?", I asked.

"Yeah, she found a way to have powers, even if she wasn't born with them", mark stated.

"But the council, wasn't happy about this", Conrad continued.

Not, suprised there. "Well then, what happened to her research?".

"It got wiped form the system, when she left", Conrad said.

"We then tried to get it back, but it was gone", Scarelett added.

She told her friends, and family, but they said, she has gone mad, cause only the leaders of the groups and their children, have powers", Amber chimed in.

"So they told her to destroy the evidence, of what she discovered", mark said.

But Lola was not happy, with all the hard work, that didn't get recognized", Conrad said.

"I think she was a drag," scarelett scoffed.

"She should have known, what was coming to her, like if I ever created something like that, I would destroy it", she went on.

"Well first of all", I said, you would first have to be smart, and we all know you are not".

"Can I finish my story?", Conrad sighed.

"Long story short, she quit the heroes and joined the outcast", "That's horrible, she was misunderstood".

The worst part is she joined the side, that we thought she would never join", Conrad said.

"She made her own group, called it the combat group, of the outcast", Conrad said.

"The powers he created were too strong, even the heroes couldn't stop her", amber added.

"What happened to her?", I asked.

"She got married, and boom the war", mark said.

"I never heard that side of the story before", I said.

But some things just don't click in my head, as I want them to, I thought.

I checked the clock and said, "oh crap, I'm late".

I got up and said, "I need to go". "Freeze", Scarelett stopped me.

"Why", she asked.

"My sister, needs me to take care of the dog, it has fleas", I lied.

"Alright, just don't forget the council needs us tomorrow, early in the morning , she said.

"You can't be late", Conrad added.

I gave them a smirk and said I wouldn't call it late, but being, fashionably late".

I took Leo's hand and said, "lets go".

CHAPTER 14

L eo and I left the scene, that I just had made.

"So", I said, "what do you actually want to do now?".

"Well I was wondering, if I could hang at your place?", Leo asked.

"What trouble in paradise?", I smirked.

"No, he said, its just my dad is gonna be annoying, also he wants me to go to a party.

"Why don't I come?", I thought, out loud.

"You want to come?", he asked. "Sure", I said, there is nothing I can really do and I want to get some info about the council".

"Ok, he said, then its settled your coming with me?".

"Its not a date, but yes, I am".

We got home and I opened the door, I saw Lucas, sitting int he kitchen, crap I forgot he was here.

"Sup, he said, he shifted his eyes, to Leo, "what is Leo doing here?".

"Well I invited him over, I said.

"So I was wondering if you would just leave the kitchen area.

Lucas smirked, and said, "whatever, see you at the party, also Leo don't be late.

"I don't want to feel dads wrath down my back, I'f you dot show", Lucas sighed.

He slammed the door and it was finally quiet.

"Alright now since he is out of our hair, lets get down to business", I smirked.

I got him a glass of water and he said, "thank you".

I sat down on the stools and he said, "I never felt more at home when I am in this house", he sighed.

I crunched my nose and said, "whys that"?, I asked.

"I don't truly know", he muttered.

Then he got serious, "hey, um, Skylare", he asked.

"What", I said, while putting down my water.

"Why are you being so nice to me?". I sighed and said,

" I already told you Leo, I feel like me and you could work together, to make this world a better place, for the outcast", I replied.

"That's why you want to go to the council?", he asked.

"Wait, your serious", he choked, on his water.

"Yes, I don't believe our parents are dead".

He sighed, and said, "What do you mean?".

"Well the heroes said, "that my mom worked as a scientist, she also created a vile, that could make a hero without powers, have powers.

" Skylares what are you saying,?" Leo said, confused.

"It just weird, because they want the world to be a better place, my mom Made a discovery that could help that.

"Yeah, it doesn't make sense," Leo pondered.

"But the real question is, the vile she made, was so powerful, even the heroes couldn't destroy her", I said.

"Leo nodded, "your not wrong there".

So, I was wondering, if you could help me look for my mom and dad?", I smirked.

He shook his head, and said, "there gone, Skylares, everyone knows that", he sighed.

"You don't know that, I said angrily, " we could all be wrong, so please, just this one time?"

He sighed, and said, "I'll think about it".

"Thank you, thank you", I said.

He smirked, and said, " I will think about it".

"Ok buddy, you do that", I mocked.

"Oh, I also got a thought, we might need more people for this operation".

"What do you mean more people?".

"Well I was hoping we would recruit a group, to help us".

"Who's all gonna be in the group", Leo asked.

I shook my head, "your not in the group yet, so I cant tell".

"Whatever", he smiled.

He looked at his watch and said, "crap, we have to leave".

"Do I need to dress up or anything?".

Leo got up and said, "no, your fine".

He hopped in his car, and left.

The car ride there was a good kind of quiet.

Finally we pulled in his huge driveway.

We got out, while rushing to the door.

The maid was already standing there, tapping her feet.

Leo gulped and said, "sorry, Mary".

She huffed, and said, "you better get your but in there, before your dad has a cow.

He nodded and we headed to the back, everyone was dressed up nicely.

I glared at Leo, he was scanning the place for his dad.

"You told me I shouldn't dress up".

He shrugged, and said, You looked nice to me".

I smirked at his complement? Then heck came out way, Mr mind reader was looking at us.

He came over and said, "song why are you so late?"

Leo rolled his eyes and said, " at least I showed, father".

Then the mind readers shifted his gaze on me, "what is she doing here?" I invited her, father", Leo sneered.

"I can see that, son", the mind reader scoffed.

Suddenly a girl and her father came to view.

The mind reader said in a hush tone, "Don't humalitate me alright".

Leo rolled his eyes and muttered, "you do that all on your own father".

I chuckled at that.

The girl smiled and said " hows it going leo.

Leo smiled and said, "I'm doing good, how about your rose?".

She leaned in and said, "to be honest with you, this party is a drag".

She then glanced at me, and said, "who's she, and why can't I smell her?"

Chapter 15

"Well, she is the daughter of Lola and Kane, Leo said.

Rose's eyes went wide, "really?", she said.

"Why is she looking at me, like that", i whispered to Leo.

Leo chuckled and said, "Shes in shock", he whispered back.

She then threw herself on the ground, and said,"let me humbly serve you".

"What is she doing?", I asked Leo.

Leo smirked and said, "Just wait for it.

Her eyes suddenly turned purple.

"What the actually heck".

"Don't worry shes just trying to use her powers.

Then she turned back to normal.

Her brown eyes, were watery now.

"Why are you crying?", I asked.

"This is amazing she smiled, the prophecy is finally coming true.

"Yeah, I'm the chosen one".

"But the weird part is when I tried to use my powers, it blocked it?", she pondered.

"Funny isn't it, I smirked, now since you believe me, I want to ask you something?"

She got up from the ground and wiped off her pants, "anything for you, Skylares walker.

"Alright this might sound crazy but, I think my parents are alive", I blurted out.

"What", rose said, "that's impossible".

"I know, just let me explain".

"Alright let me just sum up for you, my mom and dad, aren't dead".

"How are you so sure about that, thought?", rose asked, "There are so many pieces to the puzzle, that aren't matching", I said.

"So I'm am gonna get answers from the council, themselves.

Rose looked at Leo then back at me, "you sure you want to do that?"I nodded, and said, "they cant say no to the daughter, of the greatest outcast leaders".

Rose smiled and said, "I'm in, when do we leave?" I smirked and said,

"As soon as we can find more people. "oh, i have an idea ,why don't we ask Lucas?".

"Oh, i have a better idea, how about no".

"Why not?", rose groaned.

"He knows the council, and he might know more stuff about your family".

"I doubt it, right Leo, back me up on this thought".

He finally got out of his trance and said, "yeah", Leo said,"he must be really busy.

Then karma came right in the butt.

"Who's always busy?" a boy's voice, asked.

"Oh Lucas, just the person we need", rose smiled.

"No", I said ,while glaring at rose.

"Skylares needs people, so she can find her mom and dad", rose blurted out.

"What, you think Lola and Kane are alive?.

"Yes", i said, "why, is that so funny to you?".

"First of all they're dead, second of all, there should be no answer second, cause , well, there still dead Skylares", Lucas sighed.

"But how Lucas?, no one knows how, and I bet the people who do know, are the council?".

"Why would they tell you, if they are alive or not?"', Lucas pondered.

"Cause of the freaking daughter, I should have the right to know, if my parents are dead or alive, I yelled.

Lucas raised a eyebrow, and said, "If you ever want to get or even near the council, you need me".

"Oh that's so funny, cause we were just about to ask you".

"Alright then", he smirked, "ask away".

"We need you", I said, while rolling my eyes. "I'm sorry", he chuckled, "I couldn't hear you with all that eye rolling you, just did".

"We need you", I said, again.

He smiled, and said, "that wasn't hard was it".

"Alright then, after today, we were leaving for the realm", I stated.

Lucas nodded, and said, "that's perfect, I have to leave tomorrow too".

"But, I interjected, before we leave, I need to go talk to a friend.

"We meet at my place got it, the group all nodded and I said, "great".

Leo dropped me off at my place, after the party was over.

I got out and said, "see you tomorrow".

He nodded and said,"see you tomorrow.

I opened the door to my place, lily and Rob were sitting standing in the kitchen.

They asked, "how my day was".

I said, "it was fine".

"Also, I'm going to the council tomorrow", I blurted out.

I was about to walk away when lily said,"freeze, rewind, please explain to me why?"

"Yeah," Rob said, That's a joke right?""No", why would I joke, like that, I scoffed.

"I'm serious, I think my parents are alive. Skylares your parents died, they are not coming back", lily protested.

"You're wrong, the council knows what happened to them".

It's weird how they died, my mom had amazing powers, a kind of power that no one could handle".

"That's why, I'm going to the realm", I said.

They looked at each other, lily sighed and said,"are you sure about this?".

Lily came over and hugged me and said, "We support you, but don't forget where you came from".

"You truly have grown up", Rob sighed.

I smiled and said, "I have, haven't I"

Lily and Rob nodded and said, "go get some sleep, well hold down the fort", lily smiled.

I smiled and said, " thank you so much.

Lily sniffed, and said, "Go to bed, before I start to cry.

I smiled and said, " alright, good night, you two.

"Good night, they said".

I tried to sleep, but all I could thing was: Are they dead or alive?

CHAPTER 16

T he next morning was a rush.

I got up and heard Lucas and Leo, already chatting with lily and Rob, about the quest.

I brushed my hair, and teeth and changed.

I looked at myself and smiled.

This is for you mom and dad.

I walked downstairs and said, " you boys, reader?".

Leo gave me an up and down, I smirked, and I said, "you done, checking me out?".

He grins and said, "I just wanted to see you normal".

"What do you mean normal?", I asked.

Leo shook his head and said, "Youll see.

"Great, I said, while rolling my eyes.

I gave lily and Rob or last hug before I was off.

I sat in the back, with Leo in Lucas's jeep.

"So, Lucas asked, what's your plan?".

" I was hoping to claim back the leadership of Lola and kanes, daughter".

"That sounds so basic, Lucas complained".

"Alright", Lucas said," where here".

I looked around and saw nothing. "Just wait the mist is in the way", Lucas said.

Then the mist went away, and I saw rose walking looking like a girl on a mission.

She hoped in the front with Lucas, and she said," omygosh I cant wait to go back home", she squealed.

Its been how long?, maybe years, she continued".

"years?, I repeated. "Arent there portals, so you can go, as you please?", I asked.

Rose was about to explain, but Lucas gave her the eye.

"she muttered, a "nevermind, you will figure it out, on your own".

"what are you not telling me?", I sternly said.

"look, Skylares I wish I can tell you, but i can", rose warned.

"Yeah, I get that, but as the leader, I should have the right, to know?", I said. It got quiet.

Leo then spoke, and said, " you will know when the time is right, we cant personally tell you, cause thats the rule of the prophecy".

I nodded and said,"I see. It got a awkwardly silent, then Lucas said, "were here".

"Alrighty", I said, while unbuckling, "this wont take long, I promise.

I got out and headed to phin's door.

I knocked and he yelled, "I dont want your cookies.

I yelled back, I'm not the girl scout, phin".

I heard a rumble, then the door opened up.

"Hello Skylare, what can I do for you?", phin asked.

"Well, I'm heading to the council".

Phin froze, and said, "why do you need to go there?".

"Well, I think my parents are alive", I shrugged.

Phin looked outside and gave a look, "just checking if anyone is listening".

"Come in", he warned.

"How do you truly know, if there alive or not?", phin asked.

"Cause how did the heroes kill her, my mother was so strong, the heroes nor the council, could end her?", I said.

"So, what do you think about the information I gave you?".

"I think the council knows were they are, then anyone else in the realm or the modern knows, phin said.

I smiled, and said thank you phin".

"For what?", he smiled. "Helping me", I smirked.

"You might not be wrong about your theory?", Lucas pondered.

"What, I knew my theroy was not wrong, but I didn't think it would be right, either".

Phin shook his head, and said, " no one talks about, your mom and dad's death, or what happened, they were planning on destroying W.C.H together".

"Really", I said.

"Also, your supposed to be the leader of the realm".

"Then why aren't I?", I asked.

He shrugged and said,"It's a good thing your going to the realm".

"skylare, when you get to the realm, go to the council and state you case".

I nodded and said, "Roger that, Phin".

"You do want to be queen right?", Phin asked. I nodded, "more then anything".

"So what does this have to do with my parents?", I asked.

"Well supposedly your parents sacrificed themselves in the war".

But before he could finish his sentence, the door knocked. I yelled, "were almost done".

I turned back to Phin and said, "can you speed talk?".

"What I wanted to say is your the only hope, because you are the one holding the most power, destruction and skill".

"Oh dear, Brian overload I joked, too much information, and little understanding".

Phin chuckled and said,"you better get going, before the Fana take them forever, and you wont be able to save them".

"Wait aren't you coming?", I asked.

He shook his head, I cant go with you Skylar".

"Why", I asked. I nodded and said, "thanks you again, phin.

I was about to leave when he said, "Make sure you use that head of yours".

I yelled back saying, "oh dont worry I will".

I saw my group leaning on the jeep, "ready now"?, Lucas gritted his teeth.

I nodded and said, "he sure did".

"Well", Lucas sighed, "its already dark there.

"But its still morning here", I said.

"Time works differently", he sighed.

"Come on guys, we got this, what could go wrong".

"Lots", rose said, "no on really survives the night".

"Well the will be the first", I smirked.

Lucas smiled and said, "everyone in the jeep".

We all hopped in, Lucas then drove, driving us straight into the swamp.

"What do you think your doing?", I yelled.

Rose looked back and smiled, "were going to the realm, sill goose".

The jeep became a pretty cool convertible underwater jeep.

As we crossed the weird borders of the modern world and the realm.

I felt a tingly feeling.

We were back on land, Lucas was right, it was dark for sure.

Lucas said, "we needed to get out of the jeep".

"Ok ,me and rose will be together, you and Leo will be together", Lucas ordered.

I groaned, and said, "really".

"What", Lucas smirked, I thought you wanted to survive the night.

The woods of the realm are the worst, especially at night.

CHAPTER 17

"We got to the camping site.

Lucas put us in pairs and I was with Leo.

I wasn't complaining, but someone was.

Cough, cough, Leo.

Lucas told us to bring back ten sticks.

As me and Leo walked around in the woods.

I asked him,"Why don't you like me?"

He sighed, and said, " you just don't understand, do you?"No, I don't cause you aren't giving me a answer, what did I do wrong to you?".

"Cause we can never be", he trailed off.

"Explain, why we can never be".

"Cause the mind readers, and your groups don't mix".

"What do you mean we cant Mix?".

"We can never have a future together, alright so stop bugging me about it".

He started picking up his place.

I scoffed, "you think running away from the problem solves anything?".

"I am not running, I just have longer legs then you", he scoffed, back.

He stopped walking, so did I.

He looked at me with his brown eyes, and said, " you are so naive".

I looked in his eyes and said, "I know, and I kept on walking with a smile.

I knew he was starring.

He then caught up to me, with a smirk on his face.

"You really like me?"

I rolled my eyes and said, "when did I say that?"

"All I said was, we might have a chance in the future.

"In a year from now you will be the leader, and I will be the leader of the realm, soon".

Leo listened intently, to what I was saying.

Then I blurted, "we could rule together like it was no-bodys business.

He sighed and I groaned.

"Why, what's with the sigh?".

"Leo did I do something wrong, again?, you always sigh whenever I do something wrong?"

"Your not taking this whole chosen thing seriously".

"What do you mean I'm not taking this thing seriously?", I shouted.

"Leo I want to find my parents, alright".

" I know, and I'm glad you want to find them, but they might not even be alive", he said.

I was about to say something, when I heard a yelling.

It sounded like Lucas and rose.

I yelled over here, with a crack in my voice.

They finally came over and rose said, "we only asked for the sticks guys".

I took a quick glances at Leo and groaned.

"I'm taking a walk", I announced.

I heard Lucas say, "what's your problem?".

I can't believe I thought Leo might become something, I shoot my shot and I guess I keep on missing.

I keep just hurting myself.

You know like I feel like I'm doing it all wrong.

I sat down on a stump and I thought, and thought.

Maybe I could change the prophecy and make me look somewhat good.

Like why did It change? why cant the mind readers and the other groups be friends.

I sat up and looked up to the stars, and asked, " a little help would be great, I'm barely surviving this roller coaster".

Why cant I just give me a sign, prophecy.

I am dying out here.

No one is helping me.

I think they are all against me.

Naw ,this cant be, I must be going mad, I got up from my slump stage and walked back to the camp.

I saw everyone around the fire it was quiet.

I felt like I just made it awkward.

"Hey", I said.

Rose looked up and smiled, "great your back", she got up and gave me a hug.

I hugged her back, and she said,"don't do that to me".

"Of course", I said to her in a low whisper.

We smiled at each other and Lucas finally said, ok you two, its time for bed.

"We got to get up early tomorrow".

"What time?", I asked.

"Sunrise, Lucas said, nonchalantly.

"That's in like, five hours.

"Well then better get sleeping", he said, while yawning.

After that we all went to bed.

The next morning I heard Lucas and Leo packing up.

I got up put on my black zip up and poked my head out.

"Perfect", Lucas said, "were about to hit the road.

Everyone was finally up and Adam.

We had to walk on the dirt path, since we couldn't use are jeep here.

Rose and Lucas were walking together, acting like they had been dating for years.

While Leo and I , well lets just say it was silent.

Rose then said,"I'm hungry".

Lucas responded and said, "I read in a book that there is gonna be a village near soon.

"But I'm hungry now", rose whined.

Lucas sighed and said, "here I have a bar for you".

"Oh", she said, with a smile, "that's very nice of you".

"Hey ", Leo finally said, "you ok?"

"Yeah", I said, "I'm fine, why"?

Well you stormed off last night, and I think it was my fault".

"No, said, sarcastically, "you did nothing wrong".

He didn't say anything.

"Leo, this is the time were you apologies".

"Why", he said,"I did nothing wrong".

"Gosh your unbelievable", I sighed.

"Fine, he said,"I'm sorry for what I said, "that's somehow got you mad".

"You need to work on your apologies, they stink, I said bluntly.

He smiled, and said, " I just never apologies much".

I can tell, we were both now smiling.

I sighed and said, "I like this side of you".

He then stopped smiling and said, "don't get to used to It, alright.

Great, now he ruined it.

"Either way, aren't you not supposed get close with the future mind reader?".

Have you ever heard the saying.

"keep your friends close, but your enemies, closer".

CHAPTER 18

We got to the village and Lucas warned us about pickpockets.

Lucas and rose were of course close.

And me and Leo, were actually farther away.

I guess the mind readers and destruction/skill can't mix.

We got to the market and we bought some fruits.

We saw signs saying, coronation soon, for the new leader.

"Look", i said, grabbing a poster, "what the heck is going on here?"

"Well I told you it wouldn't be easy, the prophecy kept changing, so they are using the daughter of fana".

"Why are they doing this", i asked.

"They don't have a chosen one, if they don't have one, then the statues goes into the fanas hands, Lucas said.

"Wait so if there is no leader, to take over, they put a fake chosen one", I said.

"I guess the fana is forcing them to put someone as the leader, Lucas responded.

"So if I show up to the ceremony will they hear me, out or discard me?" Lucas shrugged and said, "you just got to prove yourself".

I smirked and said when is the ceremony?" "Tomorrow", rose said.

"Perfect", I said. "Where are we gonna stay for today?", asked rose.

"I have a condo that will be nice for all of us, till the ceremony".

"How many people are in the council?", I asked.

"Like two or three tops", Lucas said.

"Do they have powers?" "Well they used to until your mom and dad took them away.

Because they thought the leaders of the groups should have it, Lucas went on.

"like easy kill, kind of powerless?"" I guess so", he said, "I never thought too hard about that".

But they can talk to fana, and she has big powers", Leo said.

"Noted", I said.

Lucas then went on and on how he got so close with the council and stuff.

And rose swooning over him, like a fly to a light.

It was cute and gross at the same time, so I loved it, and hated it at the same time.

We continued are journey to Lucas condo.

I gasped my mouth open when I saw the condo.

"Lucas this is not a condo", it's a freaking mansion.

He shrugged and said, "it's quite small isn't it?" The door opened to see a butler, yeah that's right a butler, guys got money.

He told his butler to get some food ready.

We all sat down on the couch, I said down by Leo and rose sat with Lucas.

Leo flinched when I sat next to him.

"Don't worry I don't bite, geeze".

Rose saw the whole thing and she asked, "I need to know why you guys despise each other?" "Its getting out of control", Lucas added.

"Well when I was almost the chosen one, I had these dreams every night".

"What was it about?".

I don't really know hot to explain it, but you were in it, always".

"Oh", I said, "what was I doing in your dreams?"

You were all bloody, but you were glowing.

It wasn't your usual color, it was blue like your father, and yellow like your mothers".

Your eyes were very red, but your aura was green", he continued.

"What does that mean", I said.

"I know what you're talking about", Lucas said, I have studied this matter".

"That's the color of love", rose gasped

"That's the color that Lola and Kane had when they joined together", Lucas said.

"That's how they stayed alive".

I thought that the aura was the protection, on them, but in reality, it was their love, cause my mom's aura was yellow and my dad's was blue".

"So if a chosen one had a lover, that had powers it could be mixed together , and the color would make green, rose asked.

"It's all making sense now, their love for each other made them stronger in battle".

"Everyone's eyes were big so your mom and dad are not dead?", Leo asked.

I nodded and said I guess so.

But the real mid twister is what happened to them?", Lucas asked.

"I don't know but we now know what is going to happen", I said.

"We go to the battlefield, and we might be able to find my mom and dad", I smiled.

"Also you mom", I said softly, to Leo. He, smiled and said,"I can't believe we might have solved it".

"But before we go to the battlefield you need fana's consent, Lucas said.

"How do we do that?".

"Well first, we need to worry about your place in line, so you can have respect", Lucas said.

Then the butler came into the room, and said, "dinner is ready".

We went to dinner and sat down.

I ate all my food and thought, I need to get this recipe, cause the food is amazing.

After dinner we hit the sac, cause tomorrow is the day.

I'm gonna be in my revenge area .

CHAPTER 19

I woke up pretty early, but that's alright since I have a lot to do today.

I went downstairs I saw Leo wearing a nice tight black shirt.

Dang, I didn't know that he could pack so much under all sweatshirts, he built

I sat down on the stool and said " good morning".

I heard him mumble, "good morning" back.

I sighed, and said,"good enough, so you, ready for the journey?".

He nodded, and said, "yeah I guess so".

Loving the energy, Leo, just loving it, I thought.

Rose and Lucas, finally came down stairs.

"Hey, Skylare I think it's best if you and Leo finish off the journey", Lucas told me.

I nodded, and said,"that's ok, you don't want to go against the council".

"Thank you, I can see you being a great leader someday", Lucas smiled.

" I can see your trying to get some brownie points".

He chuckled, and said, "I just want to keep my head, nothing to special".

"Ok, you do that.

"Well, we should get going, I'm ready to find the truth and get this whole mess over with".

It was a thirty minute walk so not bad.

"So", I said, trying to strike up a conversation.

"No, he said. "What, but, I didn't even get to say anything".

"Yes, that's the point, your voice is so annoying, I can't even bear it, so no matter what you say I don't care".

"Gosh I said, "someone woke up, on the wrong side of the bed", I mumbled.

"I told you to stop talking"', then he did one of his signature sighs.

"Leo, I said.

"yes", he sighs.

"I'm never gonna be enough for you, aren't I?"

"Skylare, it's not your fault, we don't get to choose, our fate".

"That's the thing you, we could be unstoppable, if only you let the stupid past go".

"I'm tired of hating on you, I'm tired of this feud with our families.

"Like, why do we have to be pressured, you know?".

"Yeah", he said,"your right.

"What", I said, "I'm right?".

It was quiet again, finally, we got to the church of the outcast.

"EEk, this is it, so what's the plan?".

"Well, I read that whenever you go to one of these, you need to have statues", Leo said.

Then the council will give the blessing to the chosen one, Leo continued.

"Ok, lets go", I was about to leave when Leo pulled me back.

He whispered, "are you crazy, you're the daughter of, Lola and Kane.

"Thanks smarty pants, for telling me who my parents are", I mocked.

He gripped my arm tighter and said,"some only know mark".

"Then why isn't he the chosen one?", I asked.

"The council is a pretty FRICKED up system", he said.

"Just say your from destruction group", Leo said.

"What about you, how are you getting in?", I asked.

"I'm using magic to make myself disappear, since I'm a mind reader".

"Great", I said, "see you on the other side.

Leo disappeared and I was left to do my job.

I walked up to the man, and he said, "name?". "Sky, I said.

"Excellent, now can you demonstrate the power?", the man asked.

I punched a hole in the wall, he nodded, and he said, "welcome, you may go in.

I walked, I was now looking for Leo. Suddenly a I felt a tap on my shoulder

. I turned around to see Leo.

"Ready to go in?", he asked. I nodded, and said, "lets blow this joint".

We sat down in one of the pews.

Leo leaned in saying, " whenever the council walks in they will first do a prayer, when the prayer is over, they will ask if there are any objections".

"Then I'm gonna strike I butted in?"

He nodded, and said, "Yes", "then you strike", he said, mockingly.

"Why did they keep me a secret, and not mark?". "I'm not quite sure about that?"

Finally it went dark, I was confused about what was going on. Leo sighed, and said, "the council are being extra".

I heard a voice saying, "welcome ladies and gents, to the coronation of the chosen one".

A girl came out of the door in a wedding dress.

She looked like a bride, walking down the aisle so gracefully.

I felt a little bit jealous.

Leo was looking at her, then he whispered to himself, "they actually went through with it?"

"What, I said, in a low whisper.

That's, the daughter of the Fana.

"You're sure, that's her?"

He nodded and said she has yellow eyes.

I looked at her again, her eyes were indeed yellow, and gorgeous.

She then made it up the podium.

The room got quiet.

The council then started to talk, "close your eyes dear children".

I closed my eyes, and the council said,"I pray, to the gifted three, to give the chosen one strength, justice, and wellness, when she becomes the leader, amen".

"Now, whoever objects to this chosen one, please, speak now.

"That's your cue", Leo whispered.

I stood up and said, "I object".

Everyone was looking at me.

The council narrowed their eyes, and one said, "what do you mean you object?"

"Well, for starters she is a fake", I said.

"What do you mean she is a fake?, she is the daughter of, Fana", the council said.

"No, I said, "but it would be a shame to say that she I not the rightful owner".

"Oh really, then who do you think is the rightful owner?", the council asked.

"Me", I said, bluntly.

The council men started to laugh,"you silly girl Lola and Kane never had a daughter".

I tilted my head and said," whats so funny", I closed my eyes, then when I opened them, they turned red.

My aura was bright blue.

I with flick of my finger, blue flame danced around my finger tips.

The council was shocked at what they were seeing. Then they bowed.

The daughter of the prophecy, was shocked.

Then she said, "she enough, this one could be a fake to".

The council nodded in agreement.

She then walked gracefully towards me.

She opened up her mouth, and said," you could be a fake, just like the others one we had to deal with".

"How so", smirked. "also if you were the real on, you would of had".

Hold on to that thought, I pulled out my moms necklace, and said, "I never leave home without it, I smirked.

She sneered.

I really did just crush her ego.

I titled my head, and said, " word of advice, I'm already one step ahead of you".

She scoffed, "you seem a little bit stuck up to be the so called chosen one".

I smirked and said, " I'm not stuck up, I'm just right".

"Now, I would move before your hospitalized for a week, or even worse bedridden".

"Your choice", I smirked, "no pressure".

Her eyes were really yellow, in fact so yellow it was hurting my eyes.

She turned to the council and said,"how about we do this, we battle till the deaths.

"If I win then, I'm the chosen one, if you win, you're the chosen one".

"Deal", she said, all cocky.

I smiled, and said, "of course".

She has no idea, who she just messed with.

Chapter 20

"Why did you do that", Leo asked.

"I don't know it just came out of me".

Leo looked into my eyes and, before I could say what.

He took my waist and pulled me into a hug.

I squealed at the sudden change in his behavior.

"Don't do that ever again, you scared me, ok, I thought she was gonna end you, since she is the daughter of, fana".

I don't know how to respond to what he just said to me.

The hug only lasted ten more seconds.

Then Leo realized what he was doing.

But it was cool, I guess.

What am I saying, I was happy, Leo hugged me.

He cleared his throat, and asked, " you must be hungry.

I shrugged, and said, I'm alright, really.

Leo shook his head, and said, "were eating".

He took my hand and brought me to a fish and chips place.

We sat down and Leo ordered some fish and chips.

I was enjoying my food when I got coleslaw on my face.

Leo smirked, he used his finger to wipe if off my face.

I blushed hard, for sure.

"You better win, or your gonna be burnt toast", Leo said.

I scrunched my nose and said, "I don't want to be burnt".

I scooched closer to him, he gave me a puzzled look, but he didn't say anything about it.

"So what are her powers?", I asked.

"Well", Leo said, there's a lot she can fly, threw fire, and she has Laser eyes.

I blinked, pretty fast, thinking what he just told me.

Leo chuckled, and said, " it's a lot, but shes still young, she probably doesn't know how to use them, to their full ability", Leo said.

"Do the lasers hurt?", I asked.

"They shouldn't do too much since she is still pretty, young".

"What's her name?". "Her name is, olive, Leo told me.

I nodded, and I finished up eating.

Leo then asked, "if I was good".

I looked up, and said, "yeah, why you asking?"

He tried to think, but I already thought.

I smirked, and said, "I keep catching you lagging,Leo".

He titled his head, and said," I'm not lagging.

I sighed and said whatever, Leo," if you do that again, I'm gonna have to think, you like me, I joked.

"Me, liking you, yeah in a million years", he scoffed.

"Ok, but one more slip and I'm gonna think you do".

We made it to the arena, and dang it was big.

I went up to the security guy, and said," I'm the daughter of, Lola and Kane".

The guy raised his eyebrow, and I said,You want me to prove it, huh".

He nodded, and I punched a wall, second time today.

He gulped, and said, "you may go in".

I looked around and I couldn't find Leo.

Leo, "I said were are you?".

Then suddenly I heard his annoying voice, say "I'm here".

"Alright", I said, looking up, the sign said entry to the arena.

"This it , my time to shine".

Leo nodded, and said, "I'll be watching".

I smiled and said, "pray for her, alright".

I turned to leave, when he took my hand and squeezed it, he sighed, and said, "please don't die.

I smiled and said, "don't worry about me, I got this".

I let go, and ran in the field.

I saw olive there, smirking like she already won the match.

The council them announced " whoever winds is the true chosen one, let the fight begin".

olive attached first, but I was like not today.

She is not what I thought, she wasn't trained enough, as I thought the prophecy daughter would be. I

took a punch and she flew to the ground.

The crowd didn't like that, so booed.

I was confused since, they're paying their taxes to me, when I'm done with this.

I walked up to her and said, " what did I say before, move out of my way?" she spit on my shoe, worst part was, it was blood, spit.

Ew.

and she said, "never", she used her flippin flying powers, which I think is not fair since she has laser eyes.

I cant only use combat and stuff.

She shifted into an owl and started shooting me with lasers. I stopped, dropped, and rolled, like it was no buddies business.

Doing that moment,many times kinda gets you restless.

So I had to use my powers, I closed my eyes, and opened them again, they turned red and my aura was bright blue.

The crowed cheered cause, I think they realized, that I am gonna win this stupid fight.

I looked up and asked, "hows the weather up there?"

her owl eyes narrowed at me, she was for sure mad.

I on the other hand was not having this bird, win.

I mean the owl tried to kill me, with her beak, so I did what a normal person would to, and I struck her.

I used my new powers, and struck her to the ground.

It did a lot of damage, because she shifted into her normal demon of a self, when she hit the ground.

I ran over to her, asking, "are you ok?" She moaned trying to regain consciousness.

I'm impressed she is alive.

That big blow would have killed her.

but then again, she is the daughter of, Fana.

She coughed up blood, but it wasn't a normal kind of color, it was yellow, goodish.

Freaky huh. I don't know how but I'm not sorry.

She struggled, to get up still cough, and her clothes were covered in yellow blood.

She smirked, at me and I said, " you thought yo u could kill me, huh?"

"Yeah", I said, "I really wanted you, dead.

Her eyes turned yellow, I knew this was the time, I was gonna get lazed.

She started shooting at me, and I guess she knows how to use them properly somehow, during her unconscious state, she got good, and she got my arm.

Leo told me it wouldn't hurt, what a big, fat, liar.

It got be bleeding, pretty bad, in fact.

"Serves you right, so called chosen one, she hissed.

"You know, I could kill you, right here, right now.

"Then why don't you?", she mocked.

Cause, I'm not that kind of person, well not yet I'm not.

I'ma gonna count to three, to give up.

She smirked, you think I'm dumb enough t to fall for your stupid antics?" "I sneered ,and said, "

Do you really want me to answer that question?"

I charged at her, and grabbed her neck, and lifted her up.

She was gasping for air. and kicking like a baby.

As I held her up high, the crowd gasped.

"Oh, I'm not gonna kill her, so chill out", I yelled.

As she was gasping for air I asked who's the dumb one now.

But as I was doing this act, I realized, I was doing it with the wrong hand.

I totally forgot I had a huge gash in going up my arm.

So, now I'm scared, of what the outcome, is gonna be.

I slipped up and she used her dangling feet and kicked me so hard I thought I saw the lights.

I was down on one knee, she smirked and said, " see it was meant to be, your bowing down to me".

The crowed cheered, thinking I was finished, when I was just getting started.

I shifted my eyes to red, and I started to really glow, like blue aura was so bright I think, it blinded her.

"What's going on," she said, confused.

"You made a mistake, I smirked, and now, you're gonna pay".

I used my other hand, which was not useless, threw a big smoke cloud at her. she flew backwards.

It hit her cold heart, she feels down and she laid there looking actually, unconscious.

The crowd was no longer shouting, it was silent.

I gasped for air, as I used to much of my stamina for this girl.

Then one of the council men said, "we have a winner.

I smiled and said, " in your face so- called chosen one".

She groaned in embarrassment, the paramedics took her way on a stretcher.

I waved bye, taunting her.

I then stumbled out of the arena, walking into he halls, I leaned on the wall and slumped down.

My hands were pretty bruised up.

Leo finally found me, and I quickly got up, trying to INGNORE all the pain I was feeling.

We locked eyes, and brought me into him, giving me a soft but tight hug.

"What are you doing?", I said kinda uncomfortable, because everything is just, hurting.

But at the same time I was gonna enjoy this moment.

His heart was beating and I was confused as why, his heart was beating so fast.

He then let go, scanned my body, with his eyes, and he asked, "you alright"".

I nodded and said,"I'm fine".

He looked down a my hand, he glared back up at me.

"Your lying, sucks, he took my bleeding hand.

I winced at the touch.

When he took my hand something weird happened.

His aura turned not yellow, like his normal color, but it turned green.

Um Leo, your aura.

He looked up and he was speechless.

I smiled, and said, " I knew it, you do like me.

Epilogue

After that whole thing, me and Leo were escorted to the castle.

As we sat in the carriage, I was itching to ask about the whole thing. "So", I said, you wanna talk about the whole thing.

"No, he said, "I don't".

"Why not, come on you can tell me, I pestered.

"I'm not telling you anything, my aura must have glitched or something.

"No, I said it's was bright green, why are you denying it".

"I don't know, I got scared ok, I was scared if I started liking you, then it will ruin my reputation", he confessed.

Its ok, I said to him.

"No, it's not ok Skylare, I'm the future leader of the mind reader, also having a crush on you might ruin what people see of me".

"Why, do you care so much about what people think of you?"

" I'm so focused on what people think, of me that I don't understand what I want".

I nodded, "then tell me, what your hears wants?"

He sighed, and said, " I don't want to talk about what my hears wants, or needs.

"Well when your ready, I have ears to listen.

He didn't answer we, finally we got to the castle and when I got to the gate, I said, " I'm the chosen one, so let me in, big guy.

He listened this time, and I walked in the castle.

It was pretty nice.

It had lots of staff and they were so great.

I saw the throne and I sat down.

I know right, a throne just for me.

Leo smiled at me, and said, "it suits you, well.

I smiled, "of course it suits me, I'm the chosen one.

He smirked, and said, "Now, now, don t you start getting a big head, missy.

" I don't care what you think, I can just resize the crown if I do", I joked.

Before Leo could say another smart answer, the door opened and the three councils said, "who here is the chosen one?"

"Great I said, rolling my eyes, you're here lets eat.

I'm starving, I just did a battle didn't I.

Yes, he said, "you must be tired".

"I am, so where is the dining room?"

"We will show you", the council said.

I followed them into the dining room, when I saw the food, I became overjoyed.

I sat down, and so did Leo, but the council stood up and said,"skylare we need to discuss something with you?"

"Stop, right there", I ordered, "I need to discuss something with you first".

"Now lets talk, Lola and Kane, shall we.

"Don't you just love that topic", I smirked.

"Do you know something that I don't know, cause I'm the leader and queen, that I should know of , council men?

The council men looked confused.

"Don't look at me like that, and answer the question.

one of the guys nods and says, "Kane and Lola they were unstoppable, you know that already probably", the council man, said.

"Well without them the realm would have gone to the heroes".

"You mean they sacrificed, themselves?", I asked.

"No one really knows, what truly happened".

But, what we can tell you is, don't make the same mistake your mother made", the council said.

"What was the mistake?", I asked.

The council shook their heads, and said, "you have to figure that out, we can't tell you, my queen".

"Your parents are indeed alive, but they are frozen in time", the council, said.

"You need to go to the battlefield, unfreeze them, and there, you will find your answer, you might be looking for", the council continued.

"What do you mean frozen in time?", I asked.

"When your parents made the sacrifice, they asked Fana to not kill them, but freeze them".

"Fana saw what your parents had, they had love and hopefulness, for the future of the realm", the council said. "So she freezed everyone, who was helping in the war".

"So how do we break the sacrifice?", I asked.

"You need to go and bring back fanas heart", because the heart is the key to the battlefield".

"She gave her heart up, cause she had love and hopefulness she saw in my mom and dad?" The council smiled, and said, "now you getting it".

"Thank you, I smiled, you may be excused".

They bowed and left.

"So I said, looking at Leo, "what do you think about that?"

"I'm not sure we should do it this year"

"Excuse me, did you say not this year?"

"At least wait, until I become the leader of my group, he said.

"But that's in a year", I groaned.

"I know, he said, but we will be older, and maybe have some grasp, on what is going on".

"I'm still learning about all the powers I have", Leo said.

"You need to lead this place, get it back to order".

"We just need time, he confessed.

I nodded, "yeah, your right, time, is what we need".

"Really, he said, I thought you were gonna put up a fight?"

"Me, fight, no, I would never, and your right, we need to wait".

We finished eating and I went up to Leo, and said, "goodnight, he said, "goodnight.

As I was laying in bed I thought to myself this is your life now.

I'm the chosen one. I'm the one that's gonna save the realm, from the heroes.

The next morning i heard a knock.

A maid walked in, she flung open the curtains, like it was a broad way.

I got slumped up and i yawned.

She then wheeled in some food.

Never mind it was cement.

"What's this?" "Oatmeal", she said annoyed.

"No, I said, this right here is cement".

"Please, don't ever bring that cement to me".

She nodded, and left, I could here her mumble, "shes cranky".

"No, I just don't want to be served cement for my daily dose of food, I thought.

I then saw the dress olive wore. it had a card hanging on it.

It was from the council, it said, " You must wear. I put on the wedding dress, and dang it was cute on me.

I walked down stairs and I saw Leo h was eating breakfast alone.

I coughed, he looked up.

His brown eyes widened and he was speechless.

"You done", I said with a smile.

"Sorry, I just never seen you in a dress before".

"Really", I said, "well, I kinda have to, it's a tradition".

"You like it, don't you he smirked.

I looked down, and said" I never thought a dress could look uncomfortable but so comfortable at the same time".

he chuckled to himself. "You look cute, when your all flustered.

I blushed and said, "shut up".

The butler came into the dining room, and said, "the carriage is ready, my queen".

The carriage ride was, an awkward silence.

I was thinking about how Leo said, I was cute.

We finally got to the chaple and when I walked in I saw so many faces.

Holy cow I thought they already had one, it would be awkward to do this whole thing, again.

They walked me up the altar and said the long prayer, and frankly it was too long for me to mumble.

The prayer finally ended, people cheered and I did the awkward stance.

I left as soon as the doors opened.

Leo saw me book it, so he followed me.

I sat down at the bench, because the dress was way too heavy, and I didn't want to waist, my stamina.

Leo saw me and asked, " can I sit down".

"Yeah", I said, while kicking a stone.

"What's up", he said.

"Nothing much just thinking", I said nonchalantly.

"About what", he asked.

"Well it just hit me like a train, I'm the leader, of the realm".

"So", he said,"what's the deal, I would kill to be the leader, of the realm".

Yeah I know, it might just be jitters".

"You are only fifteen Skylare, you have time to grow, into the crown", Leo said.

"Woah", I said that was pretty wise of you to say".

"I dabble in some books", he said chilly.

"Hey, skylare when the time is right, I think, I'm try, to convince my people to make peace with yours", he said. I

widened my eyes, and said, "thank you, thank you, I gave him a hug.

I saw his aura turn green, again.

I smirked at myself.

He definitely likes me.

I let go, "So, how soon are you talking", I raised my eyebrow.

"later", he said, "lets not rush into it, too much.

Then a letter came from out of nowhere.

I caught it and I read it, it was from Lucas and rose.

I looked up and said,"they need us.

We got up and we started to run.

I don't know why, but I feel like I was in a wedding, running away from the groom.

Oh my gosh.. I just gave myself chills.

We got out of the town, and into the forest.

I slowed down a little bit, Leo looked back saying, "what's the matter?"

"What's the matter I breathed, I think I need a new lungs, cause I left mine back there".

He chuckled and said, "It's like you've never ran before.

"Oh I have run away from many things, in my life, but doing it with a heavy wedding dress, was never on bucket list.

"Wait", Leo said, " I know a spell that can teleport us".

He took my hand and said, "hold on alright".

He then said, "take me to Lucas condo", Leo yelled.

I got a tingly feeling in my stomach, and then bang was the sound, we were in the living room of Lucas condo, well mansion.

Rose and Lucas were together and they looked shocked.

"Lucas sighed, "what is the meaning of this".

" I rolled my eyes, "You told us to come and here we are",.

"Not using magic, that is highly dangerous.

I rolled my eyes," where here, aren't we?".

"Can you hurry this up, I have a realm to get back to".

Rose squealed and said, "you won".

It wasn't that hard really, I had to go against this cocky girl.

Oh, Lucas said, " dad wants to u back home".

"Why, Leo asked.

"I don't know I don't listen to that old man, when he calls".

"He sounds like a dying record player".

Leo chuckled, "you're not wrong there, but try to live with that dying record player".

Leo and Lucas were both laughing.

"Excuse me, Lucas. Yes he said turning his gaze to me.

"When a persons aura changes to green, what does that mean?"

"Well", Lucas said, " it would mean that person is falling for you".

"Ok, skylare your coming with me", Leo glared.

Me and Leo left the condo and we were back in the woods.

There was a pond where he will get transported home though.

"So I said your going home, I'm gonna miss you".

He smirked and said, "You wont miss me", he joked.

"I just said I would, dummy.

He smirked and said, "I was listening, also skylare, I'm gonna miss you".

I smiled.

"I'm gonna miss you as well", I said.

"I better go", he said, while clearing his throat.

"Wait", I said. I went on my tippy toes, and gave him a kiss.

He looked at me, and said, "what was that for?"

"A goodbye kiss, dummy".

"They still do that?"

"Yeah", I said "look it up".

He smirked again, "do you like me?",

" I don't know?", I smirked

It was quiet again.

Do you like me", I asked.

He smirked, "I'm not sure?" he said, giving me a smirk.

"Well" I said, trying to break the silence.

"See you in a year".

He sighed, "yes, see you in a year", skylare.

He then descended, down into the deep pond.

I whispered, "I like you too, leo".